Crying Wolfe

Kerrigan Byrne

From the Desk of Sir Carlton Morley
Commander of Scotland Yard
London, 1892

Eli,

My wife, Prudence, and I have enjoyed following you down the shadowy hallways of history in your quest for the Midas Chalice. Indeed, we have found a possible lead in our very own backyard. Or, rather, next door to Cresthaven Place, the house in which my wife spent her childhood. There, a decrepit hag lurked like a dragon over a hoard of treasure pillaged from yet "undiscovered" ruins in the Near East. She is selling her home from her deathbed, and some of the treasures therein have been promised to the Royal Archeological Society as well as other museums and historical preservation organizations. However, she is famous for making shrewd deals on the black market.

Speaking of the black market, I've contacts from whom I've heard a whisper of the Anatolian Sapphire being close by. I'm thinking you should make your way to the Old Country.

One never knows what treasures await...

Your friend,
Carlton Morley

CHAPTER 1

Rosaline Goode had always known that one day, this heinous proclivity would be the death of her.

She just hadn't considered it might be so soon, or from so high up.

Though she was afraid of many things—*so* many things—heights had never been counted among them.

Until this very night.

On this very ledge.

A ledge that had just done its utmost to kill her.

A wild heartbeat kicked at her ribs as she clung to the limestone bricks behind her with frozen fingers, willing her unsteady legs to get moving again.

It wasn't that she *wanted* to do this...she *had* to. No other choice existed in the matter. If she ever planned to sleep again, or breathe normally, or even be able to function in the manner of a half-coherent human being, then there was no turning back now.

Casting a longing look at her room, she calmed herself by counting the small treasures lined like regimental soldiers on the window seat. Rosaline had chosen this chamber on the fourth floor of Cresthaven Place in hopes of a better view of the night sky. London proved to be a smoggy, overcast city that never went truly dark, therefore her one pleasure, the stars, had been tragically obscured. She was afforded, however, an unfettered view of the house next door, belonging to one Lady Vera Clarkwell. Hespera House was one of the finest and, she gathered, most mysterious in the borough, but the only thing she cared about was the perfection of its observatory.

Like most grand residences in this part of London, Cresthaven Place and Hespera House were joined by a shared wall. Where Cresthaven's roof was shingled in the usual slant, Hespera House boasted a grand dome of tempered glass from which the entire firmament could be seen. The seam between the houses was interrupted by a nook with mirroring windows on the first through fourth floors overlooking a little garden birdbath below. The one decorated with a startlingly detailed nude sculpture of Apollo.

It was along the fourth-floor window ledge that Rosaline found a path between the domiciles. And so, she'd made this clandestine nocturnal journey on three previous occasions with little difficulty.

The first, after moving from their country home of Fairhaven to the city.

Second, after her disastrous and humiliating presentation into London society.

And tertiary, after the Earl of Crosthwaite's inaugural ball where a suitor had put his hand down her corset during a stolen kiss and pinched her nipple hard enough to bruise it.

Luckily, that hadn't been the most scandalous thing to have happened at said event, and she'd been able to escape with her reputation unscathed...

If not her tender bits.

She sent a baleful glare to the slick of ice accumulated

on the ledge from a leaking gutter. One she'd not noted until her slipper found it in the dark and she'd almost pitched off the side to skewer said tender bits on the wrought iron fence below. The night, of course, had been colder than most, but she'd not realized it'd dipped below freezing until almost losing her fight with a solid puddle.

Ye Gads, what if she'd been found, her broken body draped over that indecent statue in some humiliating fashion?

She'd rather be impaled on a gate.

A curious mew jolted her already frayed nerves, and she glanced down to see an adolescent black kitten padding across the icy patch as if it didn't exist.

What she wouldn't give to be a cat.

"Nova! You dreadful sneak, go on. Get back inside. Shoo!" She flapped an ineffectual hand at the beast, who'd found her ankles and wound in between them with a sure-footed confidence no creature should possess at this altitude. "Perhaps you are Orion?" she speculated, bending her trembling knees in an effort to retrieve the thing. "It doesn't matter, I can't check for your gender just now, but I'll give you both an anchovy if you go home this instant. What do you say?"

With an imperious golden glare, the kitten dashed away from her clumsy attempt to pick it up and trotted toward Hespera House.

Drat. She'd have to retrieve the adorable cretin…or perhaps she could tempt it inside once she'd gained entry to the observatory and capture it there.

Spurred into action by the thought, she kept her back against the stone as she tested each step she took. By the time she'd skirted the entire nook, she looked across at her window to see that two more kittens had clawed their way onto the window seat and were batting at a few of the shiny little trinkets she'd so painstakingly arranged.

It didn't matter if they shoved an item to the floor; few of her treasures were fragile and the ones that could break were worthless.

She always made certain of that.

Tonight, she'd lined them up and counted them fifteen times.

And might do fifteen more if she couldn't find anything else to control this...this monstrous thing inside of her.

Reaching the observatory window, she slid a butter knife from the pocket of her wrapper and poked it through the casement to lift the latch from the inside. That done, she swung the glass pane open and peeked into the dimness below.

Empty, as always.

Lady Clarkwell was too old and rickety to climb the stairs to the fourth floor, and the staff never ventured here at night.

Rosaline had always thought the precious room seemed not only deserted, but dejected.

Lonely. Abandoned.

Her heart had ached at the vastness of treasure she'd spied within, all barely given a proper dusting, let alone appreciation.

Such a room was the manifestation of her most earnest fantasies. Had she owned a place so grand, she'd never leave it. She'd spend all day sleeping in a puddle of sunshine allowed in by the glittering skylights, and all night charting the stars.

Discovering the undiscoverable.

Leaping onto the windowsill over which Rosaline leaned, Nova—or Orion—rubbed a whiskered cheek against her shoulder. Deftly, the accursed animal danced out of range when she swiped for it and landed somewhere in the gloom below.

Wriggling in through the casement, Rosaline's slippered toes found the top of the bookshelves lining the walls of the observatory. She made her way to the rolling ladder with featherlight steps, careful only to put her weight on the load-bearing seams of the shelves. Gathering the wisps of her nightshift and wrapper, she descended the ladder and found purchase on the plush, exotic rug beneath her.

Lord it was cold in this wing of the house. As chilly inside as it was out there... She should have brought something heavier than her wrapper, but had worried the weight would make her travel across the ledge more difficult.

After breathing on her hands to warm them, she extracted a taper candle from her wrapper pocket. She found the holder she used perched upon a decorative table and replaced its candle with her own before lighting it. When she left, she'd extinguish hers and take it back to Cresthaven, careful to leave no trace of herself behind.

A metallic glint caught her eye.

This was what she'd come to find...

Drawn as if by a night witch's spell, she drifted forward, gaping at the reflections of gleaming candlelight off the magnificent marvel before her.

Telescope. What an utterly unromantic name for such a miracle of modern technology crafted from the visions of a millennia of astronomers.

Her fingers itched to tinker with it.

Tonight, however...they burned with a different need. One far more insidious and undeniable.

Lifting her candle, she traversed the room, a marvelous structure with two-story-high ceilings and rows of more books than a person had years to read them. Columns and diverse display cases were crowded amongst writing secretaries, comfortable chaises, and several velvet-lined chairs, creating a fascinating obstacle course for the uninitiated. The room was part library, part study, part observatory, and might have once served as a salon to any number of societies. Archeological. Astronomical. Artistic.

A dreamy sigh expelled from her breast as she stopped to press her fingers to a glass case containing an ancient-looking map of constellations. What she wouldn't give…

Then she saw it.

Something out of place from her previous excursions here.

A long, narrow table draped with cobalt velvet cloth upon which several things were randomly strewn in disarray.

These were not protected or covered, neither were they even catalogued or arranged with any sense of care. She surveyed the chaos with a gasp. It was as if someone had dumped an ancient pirate treasure chest on the table and forgotten about it. Misshapen coins of varied colors became the ground soil out of which sprouted gleaming urns, rusted weapons and rudimentary jewelry, along with several warped figurines of mythical creatures and patrician-looking people. Decorative ornaments of nondescript origin leaned against clay *objects d'art* dipped in aged or tarnished precious metals.

Rosaline's detested demon roared.

A greedy, carnal, appalling part of her she had never been able to fully restrain thrashed and cried and yearned. It set her skin aflame and swirled in her psyche like a whisk through thick, reconstituted soup.

With desperation, she scanned the tabletop. Some things were crusted with gems. Especially the dishes. Goblets with rough-cut gemstones inlayed with heavy prongs. A large one with what might have been a ruby. And a slightly shorter, slimmer piece, adorned with a crystal clear emerald. She couldn't stand to take anything so costly.

Please. Please. Please. Let there be an item that would be—oh yes. There.

Reaching forward, she wrapped her fingers around the cool alloy of a plain bowl. It might have been intricate once, but the prongs were broken off and it had no stem or handle. The curve fit into her small hands as if it'd been made just for her. The surface had once been etched with writing, but was now faded and encrusted with some sort of green gritty substance. The inside, however, was remarkably smooth, and it pleased her to run her fingers over the rim. It was a texture she couldn't identify. Not hard like brass. Copper, maybe?

Some of the gleaming treasure might very well be gold, which was why she touched nothing that seemed valuable.

Her inner fiend released the band from around her ribs, curled up, and promptly drifted into slumber, freeing her from the untenable tension that'd wound into her bones.

This small, ordinary cup would surely not be missed from such a vast and astounding hoard of fortune. But, for her, it would mean days, if not weeks of priceless peace.

So long as nothing unduly stressful were to occur.

Turning back to the telescope, she pocketed the cup before opening the logbook beside the contraption. It had gone without any entries for quite some fifteen years.

Such a shame.

Upon the next blank paper, she wrote tomorrow's date and the celestial event to which she'd so looked forward for nigh on six months.

A little press against her ankle told her that her kitten was feeling conciliatory, and she bent to scoop the rascal into her arms and turn it over.

"Orion, you scamp," she declared with gentle reproach. "I should have known."

It took some doing to secure the wriggling bundle of fur with her right hand as she pressed her eye to the lens of the telescope. She turned knobs on one side, then shifted the beast to the other hand so she could adjust according to the numbers on the map in the astrology periodical her brother had gifted her.

Perfect, she finally decided. Now if only the weather would cooperate, she would have half a chance to catch—

With an explosive percussion, a door splintered beneath a heavy weight. Rosaline whirled around so quickly, she knocked the candle from its perch. It extinguished before it hit the ground, plunging the room into relative darkness.

She dove for the shadows provided by the bookcases.

A second, louder explosion preceded a clash and a spark just over her head.

The ricochet of a bullet off the brass of the telescope.

Someone had…*shot* at her?

Rosaline's heart dove into the pit of her stomach, suddenly unable to pump blood into her paralyzed veins.

Scurrying behind a couch, she hid there, clutching to her chest a now panicking cat who seemed intent upon ripping her to shreds with tiny, vicious claws.

A pistol? In this part of the city? Who would even—?

"You've three seconds to show your fucking self before I light this room up like it's the goddamn Fourth of July."

Rosaline froze in terror, her brain struggling to process an excess of shocking information.

The voice. Male. Hard. Dangerous. Dark. Gritty. American.

American? That explained the pistol at least.

Heavy boots shook the floorboards as they advanced into the observatory. "I let these shots fly, best pray one of them catches you before the cylinder runs out... I get my hands on you, you'll be begging for the mercy a bullet can provide. So show your face. Hands up and empty, or I shoot a hole through whatever you're holding and take half your palm with it."

Her first thought was for Orion. If she let him go, he could dash around in the dark and the trigger-happy American might shoot him. If she lifted her hands with the kitten in it, the man would possibly carry through on his threat and shoot the poor darling *and* her palm.

No. What should she do? Even if he had the self-containment not to shoot her, he'd ask questions.

Questions like: What do you have in your pocket?

She couldn't be caught stealing from Lady Clarkwell. Not when her new brother-in-law had only just been promoted to Commander over the entirety of Scotland Yard.

"One." The graveled number landed like a stack of bricks. Closer. He was coming closer with those heavy boots.

Ye Gads. Her family couldn't survive another scandal. Oh, *why* was she such a wicked fool? Why did her demon have to constantly overrule her common sense?

A nub of graphite poked her as she curled her fingers, reminding her she still held the pencil from the logbook in her grasp.

"Two."

The ladder was only a few steps away, hidden in the dark. If she could distract the man, she might make it up the bookshelves and scramble out the window before he even thought to look up.

Up was where Rosaline had hidden her entire life.

People always looked in closets, cellars, nooks and crannies for missing girls. They never looked on the roof.

"Three."

Without a second thought, she tossed the pencil over

the back of the couch as hard as she could. Once it crashed into something on the opposite side of the wall, she leapt up and dashed for the ladder.

Another shot left her ears ringing, but she grasped the rung one-handed, and fought sweat-slicked palms and a writhing cat to climb.

"What the—"

She didn't dare look back. Propelled by terror and desperation, Rosaline climbed with all her strength.

A rough hand encircled her ankle and pulled.

Losing her grasp on both Orion and the ladder, she clutched at handfuls of empty air as she fell backward with a frantic cry.

Instead of landing on the ground in a crumple of twisted limbs, she was yanked around the middle by a burly arm that controlled the rest of her descent. He had her turned around and imprisoned against the ladder with his far superior weight before she could take a breath. Both hands tightened on the wood next to her shoulders, locking her arms down.

Where he'd put the gun, she could only guess.

The pallid glow from the city slanted across half his face, painting his features in stark contrasts of light and shadow.

He was exactly like his voice. Male. Hard. Dangerous. Dark. Gritty.

Panic was making her light-headed. Or perhaps it was his scent, both overwhelming and not altogether unpleasant. Something like cedar, stringent soap, and...earth baked too long in the sun.

"Let me go." The words had been meant as an order but were released like a plea.

"Not until you explain to me how a little urchin like you got all the way the fuck up here."

Lord but his mouth was foul.

He narrowed obdurate dark eyes at her, his lip lifted

in the semblance of a snarl. "What were you after, little girl? Because only whores and thieves sneak around houses like this in the middle of the night, and I didn't purchase a whore so..." His huge, warm body moved nearer to hers as he leaned down to take her measure.

If he got any closer, he'd find what she had in her pocket.

But the cup wasn't the *only* thing she'd hidden there.

Reaching down, she snatched the knife and pressed it against his middle. "Let me go or I'll—"

"Honey, that's a bread knife," he said with a wry, caustic sound as he easily swiped it from her hand. "What did you plan to do, butter me with it?"

Rosaline's throat went dry. That drawl. Deep and crooked. Lazy almost. Nothing like the crisp tones of her countrymen. It was harsh and weathered at the edges, like the man himself.

His breath stirred in her hair as he lowered his head to say, "You want to tangle with my rough, weathered hide, you'll need something sharper'n that."

Something primal and electric sparked through her. It tasted like fear, but without the cold, metallic paralysis. The same thrill. The same tension in the muscles. A similar giddy, hysterical recklessness that screamed at her to run...or react.

React how?

Confused. Overwhelmed. Weak and trembling with cold, Rosaline did her best not to collapse into the warmth of his body. He was the danger. Not the savior.

She was just so cold.

A yowl both feline and masculine saw Rosaline suddenly released.

Orion had leapt from the top rung of the ladder and landed on the man's shoulder. The kitten stopped his fall by digging his claws in as deep as he could and sliding down the length of the man's bicep, shredding both shirt and skin in the process.

The stranger flapped the offending arm, doing his best to disengage the clinging beast sunk deep into brawn. A string of subsequent curses blistered Rosaline's ears and struck her dumb as he grabbed the kitten with hands much too large for such tiny bones. "The fuck off me, you prickly little shit."

"No!" Rosaline sobbed as he tossed the little creature aside. She wheezed out a relieved breath when she saw that Orion had been aimed at an overstuffed chair and landed on all fours without incident or injury.

The wrath she saw in the gunslinger's eyes as he turned back to her sent her scrambling back up the ladder. It broke her heart to leave Orion to face the monstrous American on his own, but if she stayed, she damned not just herself, but every single person she cared about.

And they'd been through enough.

"Hey! Git back here." Instead of following her up the ladder, he went for something on a side table. His gun?

Spurred by that thought, she dashed over the bookshelves and shimmied out the window right before the entire observatory flared with light.

He'd turned on the gas lamps. Now he could see her well enough to pick her off the ledge with his remaining bullets.

A cold jolt on her foot made her realize she'd lost a slipper, but she didn't have the time to care about that. With the nimble bounds of a fleeing deer, she made her way around the ledge with impossible speed. She would rather meet her fate at the end of a fall than from the violent lance of a bullet.

Diving through her window, she turned to latch and lock it, hazarding a look back across the way.

The observatory glowed with golden light, but no

huge American stood in relief against the glass, pointing a pistol between her eyes.

He hadn't followed her up the ladder. Hadn't chased her across the ledge.

Dropping out of sight, she drew the drapes and held her breath.

Could she really have just gotten away with it?

CHAPTER 2

Elijah Wolfe's clodhoppers barely fit on the damned ledge, but if a little girl could make the trip so quick, he wasn't about to play the part of a chicken.

It didn't surprise him to find the window locked, so he forced it open with a heavy bump from his shoulder...the one not torn to shit by a tiny demon.

He was still bleeding, goddammit.

A nuisance he'd take care of once he got this all straightened out and was able to retrieve whatever that little bandit had in her pocket.

Bending down, he crawled through the casement feet first, kicking the velvet drapes aside and leaping over the decorative window seat.

Huh. The English sure kept nicer quarters for their servants than back home, that was for damn sure.

He scanned the room lit only by a dim oil lamp, looking for the slip of a girl who liked to cling to shadows. Times like this he wished he could develop the nose of a hound; he'd follow a trail of honeysuckle and herbs right to her. The bedroom looked like she'd smelled. Summer yellows, gold, and cream, much too soft and cheery for this dismal climate.

Though the bedclothes were in disarray, he found no sign of her. Not under the bed. Nor behind the bath screen or in the crowded wardrobe.

Eli crossed to the door. Best wake Morley and the house, let 'em know they'd an intruder and a thief in their midst. The lawman could decide what to do with her, then.

He just needed to be certain to keep the Hespera House more secure, especially until he could find a specialist to date and verify Mrs. Clarkwell's incredible discovery. Though he'd already reinforced doors and windows on the first floors, he'd apparently neglected to plan for waifish maids who skittered along rooftops in this part of the world.

Who'd have fucking guessed?

When his hand fell on the door latch, a delicate sneeze ricocheted through the quiet early morning hours like a blast from his pistol. .

Eli whirled. He'd already checked the wardrobe. It'd been so chock-full there was no way an actual human could have taken refuge there.

Then he remembered how slight the little bit had been. How his hand had wrapped around her entire ankle with room to spare. She was short and wiry, even smaller than her oversize robe had initially advertised. Enough so that Eli had felt like some kind of bully when he'd realized his trespasser was not only a *she*, but would snap in half like a pussy willow reed if he handled her too rough.

Well. Shit.

Striding to the wardrobe, he yanked it open and plunged a hand back through all kinds of unholy fabric and frippery to locate the owner of that sneeze.

What he found, was a breast. Small and pert with a nipple hard enough to etch glass.

Snatching his hand back, he scowled down at it as the imprint of the shape seemed somehow branded to the rough skin of his palm. Wiping it off on the thigh of his trousers, he sternly reminded himself how old he was and that only a rank pervert would notice such a thing on a teenaged kid.

The girl let out a terrified sound so high, it might have set the neighborhood dogs to barking if they were back in his neck of the woods.

Christ, he'd had enough of this.

"Dammit, girl, I'm sorry I put my hand where it ought not to be, that was an accident. But you know what you did, and you've been found out. If you git your ass out here and take your licks, maybe your boss'll go easy on you."

A full beat went by, then a tremulous voice filtered through the clothing. "You—you can't whip me. My brother won't allow it."

Eli actually took a step back, undecided if he was more appalled or aghast. "I'm not going to whip you. Christ, haven't you ever heard of a figure of speech—You know what? Doesn't matter. Look, kid, you left your pain-in-the-ass cat, and I brought it back because I sure as hell don't want it."

With a scrape of hangers, a delicate oval face appeared disembodied between vibrant fabrics, eyes wide as a barn owl's. "Orion?"

He unclenched the fingers he'd threaded through the cat's limbs to secure the squirmy little body in his left hand. The creature made a plaintive sound, as if it'd begun to enjoy the warm harness of his hand.

Eli tossed the cat on the bed and clapped his palms together a few times to rid himself of any vermin or shedding hair.

The girl lunged forward. "I'll thank you to stop throwing my kitten, sir!" Streaking past him, she scooped the adventurous little nugget of feist and fur to her chest and took its place on the bed, draping her legs over the side. "I'm such a beast for abandoning you, Orion. I simply panicked."

I'll thank you to stop throwing my kitten, sir? Eli found himself smirking in spite of it all. Even little English criminals were kinda endearing, what with their expansive ways of speaking and their gentle, elegant accents. Back home he'd have heard, *keep your dirty hands off my cat, you bastard!* And that was if the offended lady was gently bred with no penchant for cussing or death threats.

Lifting his hand to smooth down some prickling hairs on the back of his neck, he tried a different approach. "Look, I'm not in the habit of shooting at females. I thought you were a man." He coughed around his mistake. "I mean, not when I got a good look at you, mind. It's just that girls aren't known to prowl around strange houses in the wee hours of the morning." Jesus. He'd done nothing wrong here, why the fuck was he so tongue-tied and agitated? He felt as stroppy as the ungainly boy he'd been twenty years ago.

Maybe because upon second look, she might not be as young as he initially thought.

Still too young for his craggy hide, but at least he didn't feel like he should turn himself in to the police for copping an accidental feel.

She looked up at him from where the ball of fluff had turned into a purring puddle in her hands. Those eyes took up so much of her features, round, soft, and deep blue, with long, doe-like lashes. She could get away with anything, peepers that innocent.

Probably did.

He noticed she'd abandoned the wrapper and wore only her high-necked cream nightgown with a confounding amount of lace. She was a pretty little thing, delicate and pale. Her braided hair was a lighter shade of dark, indecipherable in the lone lantern light, and looked as if—well, as if she'd been running around on rooftops in the winter and tussling with disgruntled men. The color in her cheeks was high, as if windburned, or perhaps from her own bout of pique. Her lips were—

Well, it didn't bear notice *what* her lips were, because he was too decent to dwell on something so ir-*fucking*-relevant. He wiped his hand on his trousers again, pretending it hadn't become a bit clammy. His blood was up, that's all. His body was *not* reacting to this wisp of a thing. He liked women with generous curves and the knowledge of how to use them. Whatever heightened awareness his traitorous body was having to this situation was a result of an intruder, a slippery jaunt on a high ledge in the cold, and some good old-fashioned fury at having been robbed.

Scowling, he stomped to the bedside and towered over her, hoping a bit of intimidation might move this along. "What did you shove in the pocket of your wrap?"

Her neck arched back, and she blinked up at him with something like wonder mixed with a surprising amount of terror. When she opened her mouth, whatever words she uttered were lost in a sudden cacophony akin to a herd of stampeding buffalo.

Suddenly she was on her feet, pushing him toward the window. "Go! You have to get out!"

That he heard loud and clear.

Crossing his arms, he stood his ground. "I left that little pussy of yours unharmed, now I'm owed what's mine."

"You don't understand." She shoved again, this time pressing her hands against the mounds of his chest, her slippers scuffing on the rug in her futile attempt to walk him backward. "He'll *kill* you in a blink if he finds you here! Please. Go!"

With a wry laugh, he scooped both of her wrists into one of his and held them prisoner, careful not to snap them clean in two. "I don't die fast or easy, and I'm sure he'd like to know what kind of—"

The door exploded open, and he found himself staring down the barrel of a rifle.

"You'll die hard and slow if you don't take your hands off her," said a deep, stone-cold voice in a familiar crisp accent.

"Morley?" he said in disbelief.

"Eli?" The rifle lowered, revealing a head of tousled gold hair and the winter-blue glare of Sir Carlton Morley, Commander of Scotland Yard and his friend of some ten years or more.

The girl froze. "You know each other?"

A raven-haired woman in a violet wrapper burst into the room behind Morley, followed by a lean, curly-haired man struggling to both stuff his nightshirt into his trousers *and* keep his crooked spectacles from falling off his nose.

The woman Eli quickly recognized as Prudence, Morley's wife, as they'd met socially upon his arrival the day before.

"What the devil is going on here?" she demanded, lifting her lamp to further illuminate the chaos in the tiny room.

Eli swung the waif to Morley, presenting the thief to her master for a fair judgment. "I found this little chit in my observatory slipping treasure into her pockets."

She struggled like a bunny with both feet caught in a snare. "I—I wasn't—I didn't—He shot at me!"

"He bloody did what?" Prudence stepped forward, pulling up short when Morley threw an arm out to his side to impede the storm of wrath gathering on her features.

"I shot at an intruding shadow," Eli defended. "I didn't even aim, obviously. And I'd no idea she was a girl until I caught her."

Morley eyed him skeptically. "That doesn't explain what possible motive you could have to be here...in her bedroom."

"She's like her cat," he gritted out, gesturing to the window with his free hand. "Just climbed right up and out the top window and pussy-footed it over here along the ledge. I followed her with no other motive than to get back what she took from me."

"Your story is utter tripe," Prudence Morley accused. "My sister is not a thief, Mr. Wolfe, and we do not own any cats."

"Then who the hell is that?" he stabbed his finger at the little, yellow-eyed fiend licking what was probably Eli's own blood from between his claws. "She had a name for it and everything."

Collectively, they turned to stare at the girl whose wrists were still firmly but carefully shackled in his hand.

Her complexion went from pale to a ghost-white iridescence he found a bit concerning.

"I can explain," she said weakly.

"Someone had better do just that!" shrilled a terse, operatic voice from the doorway.

The light from the hall illuminated a tall woman with hawkish features, whose plaited, gray hair was mostly contained by a ridiculous sleeping cap trimmed with scads of lace.

"Lady Brackenfeld!" Though he had to be approaching thirty, the curly-haired man's voice broke like a lad's whose balls still struggled to drop.

"Lucy and I heard what we thought might be gunshots, and then several crashes and a struggle." Hugging a shawl around her thin, sharp shoulders, she peered at the tableau with a dignified disdain only demonstrated by the elderly and the ecumenical.

Christ, what fresh British bullshit was this, now? And

why the hell did everyone look as if they'd just swallowed the wrong end of a corncob?

"All is well, Lady Brackenfeld." Prudence abandoned the lamp to the side table to gesture back into the hall. "It's just a comical misunderstanding. Why don't you and Lucy enjoy a bit of sherry to calm you back to sleep?"

The sour-faced woman dismissed Prudence's overture with a sharp sniff. "I fail to see what misunderstanding could possibly result in Miss Rosaline entertaining a nearly naked man in her boudoir with only her night-shift on."

Eli glanced down. He wasn't even close to naked. He'd punched his arms into a shirt and pulled on trousers and boots before taking his pistol into the observatory. Sure, he'd missed a few—if not most—of the buttons and without a belt the trousers sat a bit low on his hips, but—

An iron hammer slammed into his gut as suddenly, all the words Prudence Morley had uttered permeated his famously thick skull.

My sister isn't a thief.

Sister?

His fingers sprang open, freeing her instantly as he, once again, wiped—no, scrubbed—his hand on his trousers. "Look, I didn't—"

"No one is interested in a word from you, young man." Mrs. Brackenfeld lifted an imperious chin as she rejected Eli, altogether, before pinning Morley with her icy gaze. "For the sake of your brother-in-law's title, and my husband's shares in the shipping company, I was prepared to believe that he was a good candidate for our Lucy. However, we cannot be expected to abide this sort of chicanery. I mean, *really*, his younger sister dallying with such a...ruffian. And under his own roof! The absolute cheek."

Ruffian? He'd been called worse. But damned if old

rich British ladies weren't the meanest creatures on God's green earth.

Eli's mouth opened and closed like a goddamned goldfish as the girl—Rosaline?—put her hands together as if in prayer.

"Please, Lady Brackenfeld, this isn't what it looks like."

"Oh? Then please explain to me just who that man is, and what he's doing in your bedroom!"

She looked back at him, those round doe eyes swimming with moisture, pleading with him to absolve her. To say something. *Anything.*

Eli poked around his spinning head for a fix, and realized that anything he could say damned either her or him further in the eyes of this battle-axe.

Besides, they were all sorts of squeamish here in the old country, he'd been led to understand. Had more rules than a virginal convent when it came to the particulars between the sexes.

He could land them in a deeper pile of dung if he opened his mouth now.

"He's her fiancé," Morley blurted. "To be married within a fortnight."

Still reeling from the aforementioned slug to the guts, Eli swallowed another blow that emptied his lungs and drained all the blood from his extremities and rushed it to his head.

Oh shit, the room was tilting. He put out a hand and steadied himself on the bedpost. Is this what women felt like before they swooned?

Lady Brackenfeld's features may have relaxed a little, his vision was too fuzzy to tell. "Well," she smoothed her hands over her shawl. "Well, this is still highly improper. I don't know how I feel about—"

Morley took control of the situation. "Emmett, why don't you take Lady Brackenfeld back to her rooms to pour them that sherry and assure Lucy that all is well. I'll be along shortly to clear this up." He turned back toward Eli and Rosaline, his pleasant smile dying a bitter death as he glared at them both. "Just as soon as I have a word with the impatient couple."

Emmett, the lean man with what he was coming to recognize as a familial trait of wide, blue eyes, anxiously gestured out the door to his prospective mother-in-law, offering her his elbow.

Eli didn't miss the speaking look between Rosaline and her brother. There was a desperation to it.

An unspeakable fear that set his senses on edge.

Once the old woman drifted out of earshot, Morley shut the door firmly, allowing the remaining occupants of the room to visibly deflate.

"Quick thinking, Morley." Eli strode forward and clapped his old friend on his solid, steady shoulder. "But doesn't it seem like a fortnight might be a bit of a stretch for a convincing farce of an engagement? I mean, I just blew in from across the pond yesterday."

"No, Eli..." Morley pried his fingers from the rifle one by one, setting it down behind the door with visible reluctance. "A fortnight is how long it will take me to procure the marriage license."

CHAPTER 3

"Come the fuck again?" Eli strode closer to Morley, if only to make sure he was hearing the lawman correctly.

Rosaline scampered out of his path and retreated to the bed where Prudence went to console her.

Morley, a man of medium stature with the strength of a titan and a force of will as hard and unbending as tempered steel, now regarded him with a damned unsettling sort of helpless regret. "I'm sorry, Eli, but under these circumstances, it's the only course of action."

"I can think of probably a dozen different courses of action. Not the least of which is jumping out that window head-first."

His old friend ran a hand over his sharp, angular face, uncovering grooves of exhaustion deepening by the moment. "Now's not the time to be hyperbolic, Eli. This is damned serious. The Goode family has been through more than enough scandal, and something like this might just see the entire name crumble. We are really at a pivotal moment with Emmett's much-needed alliance with Lady Brackenfeld's family, and—"

Eli put his hand up. "I feel for you, friend, I do. But I fail to see how your delinquent sister breaking into my house and touching or taking my shit without my permission behooves me to shackle myself to some stranger until *death do we part*."

Prudence put a defensive hand on Rosaline's shoulder. "She's not a delinquent, she's a dear heart! Besides, her trespassing in your home isn't what forces our hands here. It's the fact that you broke into the window rather than gaining entrance through the front door like any regular person would do."

Eli's blood began to boil. "I chased this *clearly* irregular young lady across an ice-laden ledge to save your asses from being robbed! I didn't want to make a scene while you had guests, so I thought I'd get back whatever it was she'd stolen, scare her against any more crooked behavior, and be on my way. I was gonna save you all the burden of theatrics and tell you in private—" He threw his hands up against the invisible walls closing in. "Know what? I don't have to explain myself to you. What are you doing with your sister-in-law sleeping in the attic anyhow? You treat her like the help?"

Pinching the bridge of his nose, Morely answered, "No, Eli, this house was built before the eighteenth century. Our servants often sleep below stairs by the kitchens and the storage."

"Should have fucking guessed," he muttered. "Americans put our servants up top, so we don't have to climb so many stairs."

"Yes," Morley answered wryly. "I've gathered you're all about the economy of movement and output of effort."

"We're going to talk later about why that sounded like an insult." Eli jabbed his finger in Morley's direction. "But right now, we're talking about why the hell this young trespasser was in my house to begin with."

"I turned twenty-one quite some six months ago," Rosaline piped in.

"Bullshit," he spat, not sparing her a glance in lieu of keeping Morley's direct gaze with one of his own.

"I'll thank you to keep a civil tongue in your head around the ladies," Morley warned sharply.

"My lack of a civil tongue is one of the many reasons you don't want me married to one of your kin, Morley, and you know it."

The Englishman's eyes darted away, finding the ladies perched on the bed, clinging to each other's hands. "Rosaline," he addressed her in the gentle, measured voice one used for shy children and wounded animals. "I believe an explanation is warranted. Do you have anything to say in your own defense?"

Ever the lawman, Eli thought as he planted his boots, arms folded over his chest.

This ought to be good.

Rosaline's gaze was affixed nowhere close to his. In fact, he caught it in the middle of a curious crawl up his torso, starting at the low, exposed waistband of his trousers and ending just below his clavicles.

Right. The undone buttons. Probably more man meat and body hair than she'd seen in her "twenty-one" years. The tattered vestiges of his decency mentioned that he might want to do up the rest of his buttons.

Decency be damned. Covering up felt like admitting some sort of wrongdoing. And his pride was having no part in that. None. She wanted to gawk at his big, ragged hide, she could be his damn guest.

Besides, despite the window being wide open to the encroaching winter, he was uncomfortably warm beneath her perusal.

"Rosaline?" Prudence prompted, nudging her with a gentle elbow. "What were you doing in Mr. Wolfe's house?"

After chewing on the inside of her cheek for a second,

she finally spoke. "I thought the house belonged to Lady Clarkwell. I'd no idea she'd passed on."

"She hasn't," Morley replied. "But she sold Mr. Wolfe the place only yesterday."

"That still doesn't explain what you were doing there." Eli's patience had reached a limit he'd not known he possessed. And yet, something bleak in the curve of her shoulders kept him from losing what was left of his temper.

She directed her answer to Morley, as if looking at Eli caused her more distress. "I was there to modulate the Fraunhofer's Dorpat Refractor so I could observe the meteor shower tomorrow."

"The what?" both men asked in unison.

"The telescope," she said as if patiently explaining to dense children. "It's one of the only privately owned telescopes with a refractor that can see the Andromedids meteors that peak tomorrow in the boundaries of Andromeda." Glancing about at the mystified faces of those gathered, she finished rather weakly. "That is...the Andromeda constellation...not the—the galaxy."

The only thing that moved in the room for a full three seconds, was the kitten, who batted and gnawed at the end of the braid falling in a thick rope over Rosaline's shoulder.

"There," Prudence patted her sister's slim hands. "That explains everything. She didn't mean any harm."

"That does *not explain* what you took," Eli pressed. "I swear I felt something in your pocket when I had you trapped against the ladder."

"When you what, now?" Morley asked darkly. "What the hell were your hands doing anywhere near her pockets?"

"It was my hips, not my hands."

Morley reached for the rifle.

"Wait." Eli put his hands in the air in the universal *don't shoot* gesture. "Let me explain."

"You have three bloody seconds."

"Three?" Sarcasm oozed from his pores. "You're too kind."

Apparently deciding against the rifle, Morley began to roll up his sleeves. "Kindness has nothing to do with it. I'm about to relieve you of several teeth, and it's easier for you to speak before that happens."

"He didn't hurt me, or touch me in any way untoward." Rosaline finally stood, small fists balled at her sides. "Please, I didn't mean to cause any trouble. It was just so late at night, and I knew Mrs. Clarkwell doesn't ever go to the fourth floor. No one has stepped foot in that room in months, and the telescope is just sitting there. Forgotten."

"Did you take anything from the room, Rosaline?" Morley asked.

She shook her head, wrapping her arms around her middle.

God was she a skinny thing. Waist as slender as a reed.

"Where's the wrap you were wearing?" Eli demanded. "I'd swear you had something other than the butter knife in there."

"Butter knife?" Prudence's dark eyebrows creased.

"I use it to undo the observatory's window latch," Rosaline muttered reluctantly, padding on bare feet toward the wardrobe. She fetched the wrap from a basket, and tossed it in his direction.

Snatching it out of the air, Eli could feel by the weight of the velvety garment that the pockets were empty, but he made a show of checking them, anyhow.

If only to keep himself from doing something ridiculous like sniffing it.

What sort of witchcraft did women use to smell like honeysuckle in the middle of a smog-choked city in winter? It defied the laws of God and nature and he didn't fucking appreciate it.

"Doesn't mean you couldn't have hidden it away somewhere," he grumbled. Had he been mistaken? Could his body have pressed close to the ridges of the ladder or something? Was he losing his ever-loving mind?

"If Rosaline says she didn't steal from you, she didn't," Prudence insisted. "I know her to be an honest woman."

"*I* don't," Eli pointed out, balling the garment up and tossing it back to the basket. He pawed the clothing aside, pressing them this way and that before opening a drawer full of dainty things he wished he hadn't seen. "I don't know her at all." He moved on to a delicate dressing table topped by foreign feminine doodads and jars filled with shit he couldn't begin to identify. "Which is why I'm *not* marrying her."

When he reached for a floor-to-ceiling cupboard in the corner, Rosaline leapt forward, a strangled denial tripping off her tongue.

Gotcha, Eli thought. With a triumphant flourish, he unlatched the cupboard and pulled it open.

At least half a dozen fuzzy kittens spanning several colors of the spectrum tumbled out onto the ornate carpet. They seemed to sprout from another basket lined with fluffy linens placed next to a box full of fresh dirt and sand.

"Rosaline!" Prudence gasped, following her sister to the floor in order to collect the sprightly crew of cats. "Where did you get all these? Why were you keeping them in the cupboard?"

Eli looked to Rosaline, who was doing her utmost to scoop up the knavish critters and place them on her bed.

"They were living above the stables, but their mother was killed by a carriage two weeks ago. I brought them in here so they wouldn't freeze."

"Does Emmaline or Emmett know?" Morley asked.

Rosaline again shook her head.

"We've been staying at Cresthaven all week." Prudence handed a mewling white one to her sister. "Why didn't you say anything?"

The uncertain lift of Rosaline's shoulder made her appear impossibly younger. "They weren't bothering anyone. I feed them from the leavings of Mrs. Cordle's butchery along with some goat's milk, and I clean their box and fetch them fresh soil from the garden daily, so it doesn't smell. I thought if someone took offense to them, I'd be compelled to give them up before they're ready."

A disquieting ache tugged at Eli's chest. She'd kept a litter of kittens and performed all those tasks for them without anyone noticing...

Why did that seem so grim?

Morley stared, unblinking, at the balls of fluff stumbling around the soft covers of her bed making high-pitched, demanding noises. A twitch erupted in his right eye and a vein began to pulse at his temple.

"Prudence, darling," he said from between clenched teeth. "Would you kindly deal with this?"

One look at her husband sobered her enjoyment of the kittens for a moment. "Of course," she said around a ginger tabby. "We'll get this all sorted."

Wrenching the door open, Morley snatched up his rifle by the barrel before barking. "Eli, with me. *Now*."

Eli wasn't one to follow another man's orders, but he realized in that moment why Morley was a leader of men. He was so in command of himself, so reasonable in the face of chaos. Unyielding in his protection of his family, his friends, his entire city.

It was why Eli trailed him down a staircase into a masculine study rife with the scent of books, boot leather, wood varnish, and the banked coals in the fireplace.

Abandoning his rifle behind the desk, Morley strode straight to a decanter and poured each of them healthy draughts of scotch. With a rueful lift of their glasses, they both downed the burning liquid in one enormous gulp. It was only when a second round settled that they sat in the highbacked chairs to sip.

Eli dug rough fingers against his forehead, trying to wipe away a headache sprouting there. "What a nightmare," he said on a heavy breath.

"You have *no* idea," Morley agreed around a sip.

When Eli grunted with amusement, Morley leaned forward, setting his elbows on his knees. "No, Eli...you truly have no idea. You're not from here. I don't think you fully grasp the depth of the mire you find yourself in."

The next swallow tasted like ashes in his mouth, but Eli kept his movements measured as he sat back and allowed his knees to splay. "Enlighten me, then."

Morley squeezed at some tension in his own neck. "I don't know how it is in Nevada, but this is even more serious a scandal than you'd face if this had happened in any New York or Boston bedroom. A scandal like this—a man caught in a Baron's daughter's room at night—it doesn't just scar a woman's reputation. It ruins her. Permanently."

"You mean, no one will marry her?" In Nevada, women were commodities in precious short supply. Men often picked spouses they liked right out of the town brothel.

Morley shook his head. "Worse, I'm afraid. Her friends will have to turn their backs on her, or they'll be beaten with the same social whip. She'll take no part in society, receive no invitations to events, will be denied entry to her beloved astronomy societies and lectures. Businesses of repute will turn her away to avoid losing their respectable clientele."

"That's pure tripe," Eli growled. "Your country's priorities are fu—"

Morley put up a hand. "I'm aware. But I've not even

reached the half of it. Her sisters, my wife among them, will likely receive the same treatment. My children will lose their playmates. My brother-in-law, who runs a successful surgical centre, will no doubt lose some of his funding. Emmett, the new Baron of Cresthaven, will have to break a hard-won engagement. And I…I will have certainly attained the zenith of my career, if I'm even able to maintain this position at all."

Eli choked on his next sip, forcing it down in a gasping swallow. "You're shitting me," he rasped.

"I shit you not." Morley's eyes bored into his. "Though the weight of such actions are regrettably borne the most by the women, *you* will not escape certain consequences. Not the least of which are the contracts for your mines, your properties, and the paperwork for the provenance of your archeological finds. They'll all be buried in sudden and expensive bureaucracy the likes of which you cannot imagine. When those offices have drained you dry and wasted months if not years of your life, you'll have to pay more than a fair price for what you want. That is, if the deals are not somehow already granted to someone with a more sterling reputation."

Feeling a bit nauseated, Eli dropped his head in his hands. "All this because some old biddy saw me in a woman's room?"

"I'm afraid so."

"Can't we just…I don't know, kill the old lady?"

"Really, Eli, now's not the time for jesting."

"Yeah, let's say I was joking," Eli muttered, frowning into the bottom of his glass. "So, you're telling me if I marry that girl…all the danger goes away."

"Like it never even existed." Morley lifted the decanter in a wordless offer for more, like the goddamned gentleman he was.

"Hell, Morley, you and I both know I'm not the marrying kind." He illustrated this by pressing his finger down on the decanter rim, forcing Morley to fill his glass to the brim. "I may be made of gold, but I've nothing but iron in my veins. And that girl. I mean, Christ, she's so damned young."

"She's one and twenty."

"Let's say for the sake of argument that she *is* twenty-one." Eli gestured expansively, finally welcoming the numbing warmth provided by the scotch.

"Because she is," Morley insisted. "She's just small. And a bit...fragile."

"And I'm a large, hard, and rough-worn thirty-six with a birthday in a month." Eli took a few more gulps. "Come on, Morley, you don't want me hitched to your little sister. You know me. I cuss too much, I drink too often. I'm prone to occasional violence. I care for nothing but my ambitions, and I've never felt a pressing need to be a father or a faithful spouse."

"You're also honest to a fault, honorable and, regardless of what you claim, you're fair to those who wrong you and you're compassionate to those who are less fortunate than you. You're kind to those you employ—"

"Kind?" Eli lifted an eyebrow.

"Well, decent."

"I'm starting to think you don't know me at all."

Morley's features softened. "I have your measure, Eli, which is why I'm torn between celebrating the idea of this marriage and telling you that if you touch Rosaline, I'll carve out your eyeballs and shove them up your own arse."

A mirthless laugh burst from Eli's chest as he tossed his head back against the chair. "What kind of fool girl breaks into a house to use a fucking telescope?" And why did he find that as endearing as he did infuriating? "I can't have an intelligent wife, Morley. She'll hate me immediately."

"Rosaline is clever, but she's been...well...sheltered. In

fact, I would suggest keeping this a marriage in name only and arranging other—relationships." Morley studied the amber liquid settling into the grooves of crystal with undue interest. "I imagine she'd be amenable to that."

Eli eyed his friend with rank skepticism, reading a secret behind his opaque gaze. "What aren't you telling me?"

"What I *am* telling you is to be gentle with her, or I'll murder you and get away with it." Morley pushed himself out of his chair with a huff. "Pity me, my friend, I have to go smooth things over with Lady Brackenfeld."

Eli clapped his hand around Morley's wrist. "There's really no other way? We can't bribe this old cow to keep quiet?" It was as close to begging as he'd ever come.

"It will get out," he replied with absolute certainty. "This family is too influential and this gossip too sensational. If you don't marry Rosaline, these deals go sideways. Granted, you'll go back to America to wipe your tears with your undeserved vaults of money. And poor Rosaline will be consigned to a miserable, lonely life."

"Then I've no pity to spare for you as I'm spending it on my damn self." Eli swigged the rest of his drink like it was a cool glass of water on a hot Nevada afternoon before unfolding from the chair with a groan. "I did say I'd commit murder to see this deal signed."

"So you did." Morley rested his hand on Eli's shoulder, giving a few sympathetic pats.

"Only because I couldn't imagine anything worse at the time."

"I'll come by tomorrow. We'll work through the particulars." Morley opened the door to the office and followed him through it. "Oh, and Eli?"

"Hmm?"

"Best you button your shirt and leave through the front door."

CHAPTER 4

Rosaline's body had gone pathetically numb.

She perched on a velvet settee next to her brother in the lavish sitting room that adjoined Cresthaven's finest guest chamber, clenching and unclenching her hands. It took all her effort to pay attention to the extremely important conversation taking place, rather than to give over to the panic.

When would she be able to feel her limbs again?

Maybe never.

Perhaps she'd be struck so disoriented and limp that she'd forget how to inflate her lungs and her heart would no longer pump blood to her useless extremities.

At least she wouldn't be such a bother anymore.

Glancing around the room done in soft hues of robin's egg blue and muted sage, she watched delicate beams refract through the crystal prisms hanging from the lights on the wall. Better that than to witness the misery she'd caused displayed on the faces of every person she cared about.

Emmett, a new Baron and a man nearly thirty years of age, sat as quiet and cowed as she. He allowed a man of lesser rank and incomparably more influence to fight this battle on her behalf.

Rosaline didn't blame him. Any fighting spirit had been broken before they'd left the nursery…and dear Emmett's more than anyone's.

He didn't deserve this, not when he had so much to contend with. She couldn't allow her monstrous, vile demon to bring ruin to her family. To her poor, gentle brother.

No. She'd do what she must. Even if that meant the life sentence of marriage to an uncouth American gunslinger.

Across from them, Emmett's fiancée, Lucy, sat serene and vibrantly beautiful as a monarch butterfly by the cozy fire. Her wild red hair was contained in what must have been an uncomfortably tight braid, and the only impression of emotion was the way she ceaselessly twisted the engagement ring on her finger.

Morley and Lady Brackenfeld squared off in the middle of them all, their battlefield a splash of expertly woven rugs from the Mideast.

The older woman stood like a brigadier general in a lace cap. "I was ready to overlook the scandalous bigamy of Emmett's father, as the outcome meant that Cresthaven Shipping and Storage still had a man at the helm rather than a female heir. But this? *This* is too much!"

The female heir she'd referenced was Rosaline's half-sister Felicity, who currently toured the Mediterranean on a continental Duchesse's luxury yacht with her twin sister, Mercy.

Felicity had been named the heir in their father's will, until it was revealed that Clarence Goode had married two wives and divorced neither. Emmett, Rosaline, and their elder sister, Emmaline, were products of Goode's first and legally legitimate marriage. As all parents involved had passed, a legal battle of epic proportions might have ensued if Felicity hadn't generously relinquished her hold on the business and the property to Emmett, in favor of galivanting around the globe with her and Mercy's delightful Monegasque husbands.

Rosaline yearned to be with them now as she watched Morley's eyes glint dangerously in his handsome face.

"Lady Brackenfeld," he said, his carefully regulated inflection heroically unchanged. "When I said this was a comical misunderstanding, I truly meant it. Mr. Wolfe is from an oblique part of the West rife with, shall we say, charming little rituals akin to some of those our own country-dwellers cling to. Truly, this is just as harmless and forgivable as a May Day celebration in Hampshire."

The unpleasant woman scoffed. "If you expect me to believe that accosting a young bride-to-be in her *bedchamber* is some kind of godforsaken American tradition, you'll have to work harder to convince me, Sir Carlton."

Morley had donned a vest and shoes, appearing the casual gentleman, though the hour approached three in the morning. "I vow, Lady Brackenfeld, when I visited the American West, I was often privy to such strange and savage practices from our uncivilized cousins." He kept his tone light, unaffected, and thoroughly straightforward. Though Rosaline couldn't help but notice the vein pulsing in his temple. "Indeed, once I visited a town along the Colorado River where it was customary for a betrothed couple to be sewn into bedclothes by their families and left in the bed together. I'll save you the particulars of what was allowed to happen should one or both find their way free."

"Ghastly!" Lady Brackenfeld exclaimed.

"It's a backward place, in so many respects." Morley effortlessly played to her snobbery, smoothing the fine, fair hair he'd tamed with pomade before holding court with his adversary. "I've heard tell there's a footrace somewhere in Kentucky where women chase the town bachelors and if they catch them and tie them up, they get to haul them to the altar."

Putting a waspy hand to her chest, she gasped. "Good Lord, that's barbaric."

"That's America." Morley shrugged in a perfect display of helpless, good-natured bafflement.

Lady Brackenfeld didn't seem thoroughly convinced of his presentation. "Then why accept him into your family?" was her shrewd inquiry.

At that, Morley's ice blue eyes shone with a mysterious mischief. "Do you know what they call Elijah Wolfe in the States, my lady?"

"I can't begin to imagine." She rolled her eyes, touching a handkerchief to her mouth to cover an exaggerated yawn.

"They call him Midas. Because everything he touches turns to gold."

Snapping her lips shut mid-yawn, she speared Morley with an arrested stare. "Go on."

Morley slid a glance toward Rosaline, the corner of his mouth lifting ever so slightly. "I am not so gauche as to speak of money in the presence of gentleladies."

"What is one more indiscretion on a night like this?" She waved her handkerchief at him, insisting he continue.

"Welllllll," Morley drew out the word, stretching the anticipation to maximum effect. "I invested in some iron mines in Nevada with him a little more than a decade ago. And the iron mines became defunct in a matter of months; however, they struck a vein of gold, which became a veritable river of the stuff."

The woman's jaw went slack. "You're saying that loutish Neanderthal owns a working gold mine?"

Morley's laugh was rich and genuine. "I'm saying his one gold mine made me a fortune. *And* financed Wolfe's acquisition of copper mines in Utah, silver mines in New Mexico, not to mention both iron and gold mines dotting the whole of the North American continent, including the Yukon and Alaska. Believe me when I say, Lady Brackenfeld, Miss Rosaline is about to become the wealthiest woman you've ever met."

The woman blinked several times before stammering. "But I—I've met the Queen."

"Indeed." Morley winked.

Rosaline barely felt Emmett's hand close over hers in a tight squeeze. It was as cold and clammy as her own. She sat, paralyzed, her unblinking eyes searching Morley's features for a lie. She'd been able to tell that he was spinning a yarn for Lady Brackenfeld at first, but once he'd mentioned the mines, he'd seemed to be in earnest.

Prudence had mentioned Morley's money came from his investments in overseas mines rather than his career in civil service, but could he be stretching the truth in regard to the American to smooth over the catastrophe she'd caused?

The Countess's fingers trembled just as violently as Rosaline's when the old woman clutched the lace at her throat. "And...this Mr. Wolfe is to be married into *your* family, which means he'll be connected to our family?"

"If you are still amenable to the match between Emmett and Lucy," Morley prompted.

"Well then." Lady Brackenfeld turned on unsteady legs toward where Rosaline clung to her brother. "Lord Cresthaven, you neglected to share the happy news of your sister's engagement with us."

"Forgive me, my lady." Emmett bowed his head in deference. "As it is not a society match, per se, Rosaline and Mr. Wolfe were going to keep the occasion rather quiet so as to not eclipse any of our own happy plans."

"That was well done of you." For the first time since the woman had darkened their door, she looked upon Emmett with true approval before turning back to Morley. "Let's do try to keep this American contained until the wedding..."

Morley nodded.

"It would be best for both our families to avoid a scandal."

"Categorically." Motioning for Emmett and Rosaline to rise, Morley herded them toward the door. "We'll leave you to turn in again, my lady, with our apologies for the eventful night."

Emmett bowed to his future wife and mother-in-law, and Rosaline dipped a curtsy before escaping into the hall.

Nothing was said as the somber procession climbed the stairs to the fourth floor as if they led to the gallows.

They paused in front of her room, and Morley opened the door to a chorus of meows. He promptly shut it again, standing with his hand clenching the latch for several breaths.

Whirling on his heel, he examined both Emmett and Rosaline for a brusque and tense moment before announcing, "I am going to find my wife and get some bloody sleep." He put a hand on Rosaline's shoulder, doing his level best to comfort her. "Don't fret overmuch. We'll talk in the morning." With that, he marched into the shadows, leaving Emmett and Rosaline staring after him helplessly.

Emmett turned to her with an expression of helpless chagrin, his hands plunged deep into his pockets. "Did I hear...cats?"

With a sigh, Rosaline opened her door and allowed him to trail her into her room. The lamp was still lit, and a chill hung in the air from the window having been open for so long.

Pru had seen the fire fed and somehow secured the window shut and had drawn the drapes.

Drifting on legs she didn't own, Rosaline made it to

the bed just before her knees lost their starch, and she landed with a heavy plonk.

"Look how charming they are," Emmett exclaimed, crouching to gather a brawling pair into his hands and chuff at their attempts to gnaw on his fingers. "Where's Beatrix? Did you leave her in the barn?"

"She died beneath a carriage wheel weeks ago," she answered without inflection.

A fortnight ago.

The span of time she had left until she was a married woman.

"You didn't tell me." Emmett sank across from her, allowing the wrestling match to resume on her coverlet as he intervened a few times, dragging the feline attentions from each other with a trailing finger.

"You already had so much on you mind," Rosaline said. "I didn't want to give you unhappy news." In truth, she'd been overwhelmed by the myriad of changes in their situation, and the family seemed all too happy to allow her to escape to her lonely room for entire days on end.

She, the youngest of the Goode brood, hadn't Emmaline's beauty or charisma, nor was she a lone male heir in a litter of females. She was ordinary, small, damaged Rosaline with dowdy ash hair, eyes too big, and a proclivity best hidden from the world.

Nova, the other black kitten, clawed her way up the bedclothes and climbed into her lap, loudly demanding affection.

Rosaline stroked the delicate down beneath Nova's chin, her vision blurring somewhere in the middle distance. Focused on nothing. Seeing everything.

Should she be crying tears of terror? Celebrating good fortune? It was apparent Lucy and her mother would have thrown Emmett over in a moment for a chance to shackle a man named for Midas.

But all Rosaline could think of was how that story ended. How the golden touch became the greedy king's nightmare.

Emmett put a hand on her knee, squeezing it reassuringly. "You don't have to do this, Ros," he whispered, as if afraid of being overheard.

Rosaline blinked his features into focus. The thick umber waves of disobedient hair he always forgot to have barbered regularly. The boyish blueberry eyes magnified by his spectacles, gloomier than they ought to be. Observant and gentle and endlessly clever. The brackets around his mouth deepened not by age, but by years of fathomless misery and mistreatment. When so many would turn their pain into bitterness, like Emmaline was wont to do, he redirected his into a compassion so vast it strained credulity.

If there was a heart more tender in this world than hers, it was Emmett's, and she couldn't be the one to bruise it.

"Of course, I have to do this, and I should. The entire debacle is my fault."

He pushed his spectacles up a patrician nose. "Perhaps this is a sign. Would it be so very terrible if we were exiled back to Fairhaven and lived the rest of our days in scandalous seclusion?" The hope in his question broke her heart.

"No," she answered. "It wouldn't be terrible for you or me. But for them..." They both looked toward the door, the one that led down hallways of rooms belonging to seven Goode siblings in all, though most of them resided elsewhere at the moment. Rosaline's care stretched beyond the walls of Cresthaven. "Now that you're a Baron, Emmett, you've responsibilities to your tenants and to those in the employ of the shipping company. You've a fortune and a legacy to look after. You can't run from that any more than I can run from the consequences of what I've done."

His gaze was unbearably bleak. "What if I'm not meant for a legacy, Ros? We all know the fall of the Goode name could at any time be discovered. And the fault would be mine."

"That won't happen." Rosaline leaned over to grasp his hand. "We've buried it. You're marrying a great beauty. No one will know."

"We'll know."

She *did* know.

Knew that Emmett felt affection for other men, rather than women. He'd developed an attraction to a friend at the age of nine and had been institutionalized for it. Once he'd convinced the doctors he'd been cured, they'd returned him home at the age of sixteen, a sad and broken boy. Lonely and troubled, afraid of any sort of connection with other men, friendly, filial, or otherwise. Over the years, it'd become apparent his predilections hadn't changed, but he'd zealously masked them.

Emmett had turned somber and introverted beneath the scathing control of their uncle and steward, who'd somehow erased any record of his incarceration. However, they were all aware that the recent death of their uncle might yet prove disastrous. In the event that damning paperwork was ever uncovered, it was imperative that Emmett marry and produce an heir.

So he could deny who he really was in order to maintain his freedom.

Rosaline cupped his cheek, one still not capable of producing a full beard even at seven and twenty. His lot wasn't much better than hers.

They'd both be consigned to loveless marriages.

Good lord. She was going to have a *husband*. She was going to have to—to do what husbands and wives did.

She prepared to cringe with revulsion, but it wasn't as forthcoming as expected.

"Emmett..." she ventured, drawing little whorls into Nova's long, wispy coat with a fidgeting fingertip. "Do you find Mr. Wolfe handsome?"

His head snapped up and his brows drew together in approbation. "Don't ask me such cruel questions, Ros."

"I'm not meaning to be cruel. I just..." She leaned closer, pressing her forehead to his. "We could whisper about it if you wish. I don't mind that you are—who you are."

"What I am, you mean?" He winced as if to cringe away from himself, turning from her.

"No." She tightened her grip on his hand. "*Who* you are... I think that who one loves is part of who one is."

His throat bobbed with a difficult swallow, then another, his eyes never leaving the brawling kittens as he said, "I wish I could tear that part of me out. That I could be who everyone expects me to be."

She cupped his jaw and let the moisture gathering in her lashes fall down her hot cheek. "I wish you didn't have to."

"None of that," he crooned, extracting a handkerchief from his shirtsleeves to wipe at her tears. "He *is* handsome, your Mr. Wolfe." Emmett breathed the words like a gentle confession. "I...I liked the way his eyes creased at the corners, and the exaggerated shape of his jaw. He has a rather—I don't know—vital way about him, does he not? Strong and um—well, he's the sort that would be capable in a crisis now, wouldn't he?"

"I suppose you're right," she agreed, the vise around her ribs loosening one notch. "Not as good a shot as Morley, I'm thankful to note."

That summoned a wry smile to her brother's lips. "I'm glad, too; I couldn't imagine carrying on without you." Instantly, he sobered. "Did you take something from him, Ros?"

She gulped in air once. Then again. Wringing her hands in her lap. "I-I…did."

"Oh, Rosaline."

"It was only this." She rushed to where she'd shoved her treasures beneath the fluffy blankets in the kitten basket and extracted the odd half of a goblet. "You should have seen the mountain of treasure spread throughout the observatory. I didn't think it'd be missed."

"Still, you should return it."

Rosaline couldn't look up from the cup clutched in her clammy, frigid fingers. She couldn't face the pitying censure she knew filled his gaze. Her voice was unidentifiable as she pulled it from the rotting grave of her undying shame. "I know."

"What made you do it this time?" Emmett's voice was gentle as it was long-suffering. "Was it Lady Brackenfeld? She's been a rather terrible houseguest."

Rosaline nodded, knowing her tolerant siblings didn't understand her dreadful tendency any more than she did. "I—I hate that she's going to be part of the family. I hate that she's unkind and domineering to you. She reminds me of mother."

"I can't say that comparison hasn't crossed my mind," he muttered.

"At least you and your wife will have that to commiserate over… Poor Lucy."

"Poor Lucy in so many ways." Emmett reached down for the calico kitten who seemed unable to climb the coverlet as her more enterprising siblings had. Kissing her downy head he confessed, "I'll never be able to love her."

"I'll never be able to love Mr. Wolfe. Eli…" Her husband's name was going to be Eli.

Elijah Wolfe.

Mrs. Rosaline Wolfe.

"You could try, you know."

She looked over at him, aghast. "Emmett, what are you saying?"

His shoulder lifted. "It's not the worst thing I can imagine, having a man built like that to stand between you and the rest of the world."

She paused, considering his words.

He *was* alarmingly large, her intended. Hard and scarred and dusted with dark hair. He didn't just occupy space, he claimed it. Claimed it with his wide shoulders and his deep chest. A chest chiseled with grooves and sculpted with swells that sophisticated British men didn't possess. Indeed, there was nothing at all elegant about him. His hands were rough and square, both his palms and his voice heavy and abrasive as brick.

Emmett lay back on her bed with what she could only identify as a dreamy sigh. "Doesn't it seem like he could protect you from—well, from just about anything?"

Rosaline joined her brother, staring up at the canopy as little creatures romped and clawed their way over and around them. "It does," she agreed softly.

But who would protect her from him?

CHAPTER 5

Eli couldn't remember the last time he'd so viciously wanted to shoot something. Or hit something. Or snap something over his knee and beat something else to death with it before lighting both things on fire and sending them to hell.

He'd never been so happy to return to a quiet, empty house.

After a late morning with Morley and their lawyers—whom the Brits called solicitors, though he could find exactly nothing solicitous about them—he'd had his own business to contend with.

Contend being the operative word.

Land deals sure meant the world to people who called themselves lords, and even more to those lords whose families had owned said land for hundreds of years. Sometimes longer.

Apparently, after business, men in this town went for "a bit of sport," which sure as hell meant something different than where he was from.

Though Eli did his level best to enjoy a night of drinking, gambling, and carrying on with flirtatious women drenched in heavy gems and perfumes, he just...couldn't.

It wasn't that he felt any sense of fidelity to his bride-to-be. He'd never even had a proper conversation with her.

He was just...getting too damn old for this shit. The noise and the odors and the vibrant colors, he'd once found them dazzling. Had been drunk on the fact that he could walk into a room and buy anything, or anyone, in it. Power was such an effective intoxicant. Wealth, a heady seduction.

It was freedom.

Or so he'd once thought.

Yanking away the silk noose at his neck, he had one button of his collar thrown before he'd reached the first-floor landing of Hespera House. Flexing and stretching his right hand, he examined the few superficial cuts on his knuckles. They'd be swollen and sore tomorrow.

Though not as sore as that Viscount's smarmy face.

Eli'd never met the man in his life, and still the worthless lordling had the gall to sneer at his 'crass American money.' He'd mocked Eli's callused palms and his sun-baked skin, as if his own limp, smooth lady-hands were something to be proud of. Proof he'd never worked for anything he owned. When unable to get a rise out of him, the young man, surrounded by a pack of pathetic mates, announced Eli's engagement to a club full of men like a fucking matron clucking gossip at a church social.

And here he thought news traveled fast in small towns.

Apparently, London had a few telephones installed, and it seemed the days a man could outrun what was said about him were over forever.

Eli had held his temper. Held it like a fucking champion until the buck-toothed bastard insinuated that the youngest sister of a country Baron who had to work as a shipping entrepreneur might just be unrefined enough to deserve the likes of him.

Back in Nevada, you try and take digs at a man's work

or his woman? You sucked the end of his barrel until he ejaculated lead and gunpowder through the back of your skull.

The lad was *lucky* to have escaped with only a broken jaw.

The way his compatriots scampered, Eli imagined they'd not realized the complete height and breadth of him until he was scowling down at them, itching for another face to plant his fist in.

Or they'd underestimated his willingness to commit physical violence when dining at a table with three members of Parliament.

Eli conquered the second- and third-floor stairs two at a time, looking forward to a hot soak and—

What the—?

A seam of light from beneath the door to the observatory broke his step.

He checked his watch. Ten thirty. Mrs. Clarkwell barely made it to her wheelchair these days, let alone to visit the treasures he promised she could come and stare at any time.

There was a fortune in archeological finds in there he was itching to catalogue just as soon as the professor and the appraiser could get their collective asses by to tell him if it was even worth the trouble.

Had someone heard about the find? Someone who'd known he wouldn't be home tonight?

Creeping toward the room, he pressed his ear against the wood paneling, hoping to ascertain just how many people he needed to expel from his house.

And possibly from this world.

A soft, melodic hum vibrated through the door, husky, lyrical, and…female.

Eli pulled back, glaring at the heavy wood as if he could burn through it to see the little vixen on the other side.

She wouldn't.

Eli threw the door open with every bit the amount of force he'd used when this senseless woman had invaded his house—his fucking life—not twenty-four hours ago.

What he found was entirely different scenery than before, that was for damned sure. She was dressed, for one. And the lights were blazing as if she wasn't even trying to hide her presence this time.

Producing a little *eep* of surprise, Rosaline Goode whirled around, bumping the business end of the telescope with her elbow.

"Drat," she muttered, dramatic brows lowering over a look of mild accusation. "I'd only just calibrated the new coordinates to the—"

"Tell me I'm not engaged to a lunatic," he gritted out, unable to tear away his death grip on the door latch. "*Tell me* you didn't *break into my house* after last night's calamitous fiasco and—"

"I didn't!" She picked up the big leather logbook on the writing table next to the contraption and hugged it to her chest as if it'd block any incoming bullets. "I called upon you this afternoon to ask permission, but as you weren't here, I obtained it from Mrs. Clarkwell. You can ask her, if you like. I wish I'd known she wasn't the crotchety old witch she was reputed to be. Would have saved the both of us a great deal of troub— Why are you looking at me like that?"

He couldn't imagine what a fool he seemed. His jaw gone slack. His eyes fixed and unblinking. Arms hanging like two wet noodles at his sides as he gawked at the woman for what felt like the first time.

Had she been this fucking beautiful last night?

He'd not allowed himself to notice.

Her hair was piled high on her head in some intricate style held together by a feminine magic that frankly amazed him. It wasn't a vibrant color, or even an identifiable one. Somewhere in between dark honey and light oak, if he had to take a stab at it. An almost unnatural sheen rippled in the light as she moved, turning the few loose locks down her back into a waterfall of satin.

Her eyes were so dark a blue, he had to take several steps closer to properly appreciate the color. He'd had a verbose boss once, that might have called her eyes mercurial.

A simple white blouse was tucked into an elegant skirt of fetching blue and green plaid, which matched the cravat knotted below the high-necked lace of her collar. Little pearls bobbed from her ears, obviously paired with the broach that fastened her cravat to the blouse.

She looked like a schoolteacher.

Like a woman.

In proper lighting, he conceded that her features appeared more elfin than immature, though she was still painfully young.

Fifteen years younger. Holy fuck.

It wasn't unheard of, he supposed. Rich old men took young wives all the time. And yet, it'd always seemed so ridiculous to him. Did they fool themselves into thinking such a pretty young thing was actually attracted to them? Or did they just not care, enjoying the fact that they'd bought a lovely toy to legally bed as they pleased?

Either thought had always turned his stomach. He'd considered the practice pathetic.

And yet here he was. A man with silver threads in his hair about to take on a wife who'd not been a woman for very long.

What a mess. What a goddamn—

"Please don't make me go." Her fervent plea reminded him she'd been waiting for an answer as he stood there drooling like the town idiot with a fresh head wound.

Apparently discerning he was unarmed, she abandoned the book to the table and crossed the dais upon which the telescope was mounted to entreat him further. "I figured, the damage has already been done, does it hurt anything if I watch the Andromedids?"

Remembering to inflate lungs starved for air he replied, "It don't hurt nothin'. I mean—anything." Damn it, he'd spent more than ten years fixing his Western diction. Using the correct words instead of the plunky patois he'd learned in the mines.

She made him forget himself.

And in offering a slight smile, damned if she didn't steal his breath twice in as many minutes.

He glanced away, his gaze finding the table upon which the treasure was kept, covered now since her last intrusion. The cover was undisturbed, the trap he'd set still in place.

She truly just wanted to use the telescope. It made sense, he supposed. She came from a wealthy, titled family. Granted, not as wealthy as him, but she needed for nothing.

Perhaps she was different than—

"Do you want to see?" she asked, eyes sparkling.

He blinked. "See what?"

"The meteor shower." Motioning to the telescope, she bustled back over to it, bending slightly to press her eye to the lens and to fiddle with a few knobs. "I just have to position the lens back in the right place."

Eli had never lived with a woman before. Had never stood still long enough to watch one go about her business. Sure, he'd enjoyed a romp with a few—okay, dozens. And he'd had friendly interactions with almost all of them.

But this was different.

He wasn't kicking open a door with his belt half undone, ready for a romp; he was looking at his fiancée.

He enjoyed the way the slight train of her skirt swished along the shiny wood floors. He liked the wide belt she'd cinched around her startlingly small waist. The little gather of frills at the cuffs of her shock-white blouse. He was arrested by how her feet never really seemed to touch the ground, and the graceful way her wrists and hands moved with deft skill. Like every gesture was a dance.

She reminded him of a hummingbird. Quick bursts of motion interspersed by floating, ethereal pauses. A creature so tiny and shy she was easy to overlook, but if you were allowed close enough, you discovered feathers and features unmatched in exceptional and vivid beauty.

Lord, if she turned him into a poet, he'd eat his own bullets.

And yet…was it a terrible idea to introduce himself to the woman he was about to marry?

To learn about her, as well?

"Never seen more than a shooting star," he muttered, shoving his fists in his pockets to hide the evidence of violence as he meandered to the dais.

"Then you've observed a meteor," she explained, her back still to him as she focused on the contraption. "They're chunks of rock and metal believed to be broken off large asteroids and burned up in our atmosphere. So they're closer to us than even the moon. Some of them find their way to the earth's surface and those are called —" Suddenly she straightened as if someone had poked her in the back, whirling to face him. "Oh dear. Forgive me. It wasn't my intention to condescend. I—I forget myself sometimes."

Eli cocked his head. "Forget what?"

"That…" She hesitated, her eyes darting quickly as if searching for the right words. "That men aren't fond of being instructed by a woman. Of course, you knew about meteors already."

"I don't know anything about meteors." Eyes narrowing, Eli wondered why she looked so pale. So panicky.

"I've spent most of my life under the ground, picking the earth apart to find her alloys. Never had much use for the sky other than to know the time of day or night or the weather, I guess."

"Oh, Mr. Wolfe, that's so sad."

Where he came from, you punched a man for pitying you. It was something to avoid at all costs. But the look of pure compassion on *her* face melted some sort of tight, hard tension from his shoulders and tugged at something beneath his ribs.

"Well anyway..." He rested one foot on the step of the dais, leaning on the railing that encapsulated the telescope's domain. "Most of the useful shi—er—stuff I know, I learned from women. So, I'm not particular about where my information comes from, gender-wise, anyhow."

She regarded him warily. "Then you are very different from the men in my family, sir."

"You mean Morley?"

She tugged at the lace cuff of her sleeve, worrying it idly. "I don't know Morley terribly well. I—I wasn't raised with his wife. He seems to know just about everything there is to know about everything, so I can't say I've ever tried to explain much to him. I was more referring to my father and...and my uncle who raised us after Mother passed."

A prurient curiosity tempted him to ask, "Your father's death caused quite a scandal, I hear. Bigamy and fraud. Two families kept secret from each other. How many siblings do you have, exactly, and where do you fit into the equation?"

At his query, all that was open and vibrant about her changed. She shuttered the windows and closed the storm doors, her eyes opaque and her features devoid of expression as she stared past him. "I'm the youngest of seven."

He let out a low whistle, trying to keep it nonchalant. "Always wondered what a big family was like, guess I'm going to learn quickly. Tell me about them. What would we have in common?"

Her mouth fell open. "I'm sorry?"

"One thing I learned in business was that it helps to find familiar ground with people, something to compliment them on and to discuss at events. Marriage is essentially a business contract. A merger of two families. Besides, if they're all going to be at our wedding, I'll need something to converse with them about."

An adorable crease appeared in her forehead as she seemed to ponder both him and his request with equal fervency. "Well... The Eldest is Honoria, *Nora,* we call her, is married to Dr. Titus Conleith, one of the most celebrated surgeons in the world. You should very probably donate to his surgical centre, and all you must do to get Honoria's favor is compliment their son, William. He's the light of their lives."

Eli's lip quirked. "That I can do, who else?"

"Emmaline is still at Fairhaven at present, looking after animals and interests there, but she'll be along for the wedding, I'm certain. Her favor is not easily won, but she's as loyal a person as one can be and is mad for horses, if you know much about them."

"I guess I know more about them than I do about stars and meteors," Eli shrugged. "I'll bet she can teach me something new."

That earned him a look of cautious approval, which lit some sort of glow deep in his belly.

"You know Pru and Morley," she continued, wrinkling her nose as she did some calculations in her head. "I don't suppose there is time for the twins, Felicity and Mercy, to return with their husbands, Gabriel and Raphael Sauvageau."

"Wait, you're telling me twins married brothers?"

She nodded, smiling fondly. "Not just brothers, former gangsters and smugglers from Monaco. They've retired now, as I understand it, and are happy to lavish their fortunes and their favors on their wives. Mercy is a strong-willed woman with an enormous heart and a penchant for investigation. Felicity keeps to herself and her books, though she's lovely company once she gets to know you. She's also endlessly generous."

"I understand she willingly gave up her inheritance to your brother, Emmett," he mused. "Never heard of anyone doing something like that."

She shook her head as if still trying to make sense of it. "Nor I."

"Your brother seemed..." Eli remembered back to when the clan had found him in her bedroom. The wiry fellow with a pretty shape to his face and with eyes as soft as his sister's. Man was a Baron. He ran one of the largest and most profitable shipping companies in the whole of Europe and could barely look anyone in the eye. "Shy," was the only word he could come up with.

Rosaline's expression tightened with a defensiveness he'd not expected. "He's studious and brilliant, elegant and soft-spoken and, most importantly, he's kind. I very much wish more men were of his ilk. He's had to face unimaginable adversity because of what our father did. The shame he brought..." She looked down, her expression coloring. "People can be so cruel. I'm sorry you'll be likewise blighted by our alliance."

"Hey." He stepped up onto the dais and went to her, tucking a finger beneath her chin and lifting her face to his. "I've got nothing against shy folks, so your brother and I are going to get along just fine."

A mysterious moisture turned her eyes luminescent as she valiantly fought it. "I—I hope so."

"And as for the other thing," he continued, stronger this time. "No wife of mine is going to look down in shame, you got that? I realize scandal is a powerful tool in this country, but you're under my protection now. I'm tough enough to take whatever the gossip mill spews out, and I'll rip out the tongue that speaks against you."

It seemed to astonish her just as much as it did himself how fervently he spoke the words.

How ardently he meant them.

"I-I hope that won't be necessary, Mr. Wolfe." Her throat worked around a swallow before she extricated herself from his fingers and turned to the table upon which the telescope's logbook sat. With stiff, efficient motions, she flipped open the pages and became absorbed with some numbers in arrangements he couldn't begin to identify.

He watched her withdrawal with a pensive regret that bordered on diffidence. Men like her brother wouldn't say shit like he did. Studious men—elegant, brilliant, soft-spoken...kind. Eli was none of those things.

It wasn't like he didn't understand that some women found him appealing, but they were largely frontier women. The hearty kind that judged a man's desirability on how well he could build a fence rather than turn a waltz.

The rules here were different.

She was different.

As if sensing the intensity of his regard, she glanced aside at him. "Erm...Do you have siblings, Mr. Wolfe?" Her question was a not-so-subtle attempt to break the awkwardness that'd bloomed between them, and he was happy to oblige.

Looking away, he tamped down on a surge of familiar pain.

"Nah." He leaned his hip against the table, doing his best not to crowd her as he watched her check and recheck the measurements he'd messed up when he'd startled her. "It's just me in the world."

"Your upbringing must have been rather lonely, then," she said distractedly, making a neat notation in a margin.

"It was fuc—I mean—pretty crowded, actually," he chuckled. "See, my pa was killed in the Civil War and my ma went west with a wagon company. She died of pneumonia not two years after, which is how I ended up working in a Nevada iron mine at ten years old. I slept in a bunkhouse with twelve other boys and men and never had a moment of goddamn—er—darned peace and quiet."

Somewhere in his explanation, she'd quit writing, her pencil frozen over the paper. Once he finished, she arched her graceful neck to look at him, her chin touching her shoulder. "I don't mind if you curse, Mr. Wolfe, if that is your way."

He had the most ridiculous notion to squirm beneath her direct gaze. "I should watch my mouth around ladies," he muttered.

Her shoulder lifted, and she tilted her head in a pose most alluring. "Not on my account. I find it sort of...charming."

A bark of mirth escaped him. "Now I know you're lyin'."

"Well, let us say it's refreshing," she amended. "We women are so cossetted, left so far outside the realm of men. I often wonder what they talk about in their smoke-filled rooms while swirling their brandy or port. What forbidden words they say to each other."

Eli pulled a face. "You...probably don't want to know. You'd either be bored or disgusted."

"I'm not easily bored," she informed him.

"Must be nice. I've always got to be doing something or I go mad."

"You don't sleep?"

"I sleep fine. I just exhaust myself first."

She regarded him quizzically. "What do you do to rest, then? To relax?"

He shook his head, trying to remember the meaning of the words. "I'm not sure I'm good at relaxing. An easy day for me is working from sunup and allowing myself to quit at sundown. That's how money is made in America. Here, too, these days."

"I've—I've heard you've amassed plenty." She put her pencil down, a pretty peach blush spreading over her cheeks. "Morley said they call you King Midas."

"Just Midas," he snorted. "We got no kings where I'm from."

"I wonder what that's like."

"It's fine, I guess... I mean, there are always captains of industry. Power is forever up for grabs. And those with the money have the power, so someone's always waiting in the wings to take it from you. To steal or siphon what you have for their own gain."

Both her brows and her lips tilted down. "Sounds...exhausting."

"It can be," he shrugged.

"Well, perhaps since you'll be a married man, you can take up a relaxing hobby of some sort." She turned this way and that, as if looking for an extra idea that might have dropped on the floor. "Perhaps you might attend lectures on geology since you are so intent upon what is found in the earth. Or even astronomy if you find that you fancy it."

Sounded like a great way to work a nap into his day.

Eli's mouth twisted as he paused before replying. He was too rich to care what people thought. Too ambitious to mind what they felt. So why did he hesitate to tell her the truth? Because he wanted her approval? Wasn't much a call for that now. If he put on airs and graces, he'd only disappoint her in the future when she discovered what he really was. "I don't know if I'd do so well at educational pursuits, seeing as how I have no education to speak of."

She lifted a hand to her mouth. "You never went to school?"

Scratching at an itch behind his ear, he shifted uncomfortably. "I learned my letters and numbers well enough, but not so much in a schoolroom. When other kids went, I had to work to keep myself fed."

"Oh. I—I'm so sorry." Her gaze broke away, and she chewed on the inside of her cheek as if doing so might save her from an uncomfortable conversation.

Or an unwanted marriage?

God, they were as unsuitable as the proverbial fish and bird. He'd spent his life in the dirt and she with her head in the clouds. No, further than that. The stars.

With a giant sigh, he motioned to the telescope. "Show me what's so amazing up there that you'd risk your life and freedom to watch it."

Closing one eye, she checked the lens and broke into the most genuine smile he'd ever seen. "This is perfect timing. The Andromedids are so active! I think the shower is peaking just about now." She lingered over the lens, tendrils of her hair sliding over her shoulder as she bent forward. "Extraordinary. I've never seen it like this."

Straightening, she beckoned to him with several flaps of her hand. "Come. Come. Bend here and use your dominant eye, as it'll blink less. Careful not to bump it too hard. Here you are. That's the way."

As he levered at the waist, he had to bend down much further than she did to press his eye to the scope. Once he'd positioned himself, her hand fluttered like a moth over his shoulder blade. As though she wanted to encourage him but was uncertain where to land.

He found his back ever so slightly arching toward the touch, much like a cat might search for a stroke.

Whether she meant to or not, her hand splayed just behind his shoulder, and his entire being became focused on the place where she touched him. A light touch. Maybe one she was unaware of.

He couldn't see her to tell. But with the tense and twitching muscles in his back, he could make out the delineations of each individual finger. Could sense some sort of energy arcing over his flesh, expanding from where she touched down his spine and landing in his cock.

From his shoulder blade. His goddamned motherfucking perfectly proper shoulder.

Jesus tap-dancing Christ, what was the matter with him? He'd barely been this randy as a teen. Hell, it'd been at least twenty years since he worried that a stiff wind and a soft touch would make him come in his trousers.

"What do you think?" she pressed, tapping his back like one of her enthusiastic kittens. "Isn't it extraordinary?"

Oh. Right. Shit. The stars—er—meteors. Focusing his eye into the lens, he looked up into the rare, clear night sky. It didn't look much different through a scope. Just closer. It wasn't disagreeable or anything, but he couldn't see the big deal—

"Holy shit." He caught his breath as a bright orb with a definitive tail streaked across the scope. Another to the left. Two in tandem. Then a barrage of maybe five falling and glowing and burning out like a brilliant sprinkle of rain. "There are so many."

"And the Andromedids is one of the lesser events. Just wait until next month when the Geminids are visible... You'll never be the same."

He could say that about tonight. Right now. A shift was taking place inside him, nudged along by the soft pressure of her hand.

Eli remembered something. Something he'd buried away for several years as he'd done his level best to wrestle an entire industry from the clutches of greedy men who would see their employees die before their profit margins were lowered.

"I did look for sky when I was a boy," he murmured. "For the stars. After a long day down in the mine digging deep enough to reach the ninth circle of hell and nearly shitting myself each time I heard a rumble. Wondering if I'd be buried again before the sun had a chance to shine on my face. After breathing in the Sulfur, sweat, dust, and God knows what else. A dozen men would climb into a lift, and we'd turn our faces to the sky. Once we reached the surface, we'd stand there for a long time. Breathing the air. Feeling safe knowing that the sky wouldn't fall on us. Except here it is, doing just that."

She didn't respond immediately, and he didn't much care as he gazed into the glass, watching the lovely event in brilliant intervals.

"We're just lucky, I suppose, that the sky falls so far beyond our reach," she murmured.

"Do they know how far?"

"Actually, yes. Though these showers are sort of optical illusions. You see, the meteors are close enough to enter our atmosphere, but the stars behind them are light-years away."

"What years, now?" He sent her a quizzical look before reclaiming the lens. He didn't want to miss one. "That makes no sense."

Her voice became dreamier, further away as if she'd lifted her head to gaze out the observatory ceiling. "Did you know that when you're looking into the sky, you're also looking at the past?"

He shook his head, following a particularly interesting streak in a strange and synchronous cluster.

"Some astronomers believe that the stars we see now, existed as we see them at least five hundred light-years ago. A light-year is the distance they measure in the time it takes for light to move through space in a year. Can you imagine time as distance?"

He furrowed his brow. "Not until today."

The hand on his shoulder increased pressure and he'd the sense she'd bent closer. "Directly in the middle of your lens, you'll see a constellation of overlapping stars that looks like a woman standing with chains at her wrists that connect to nothing. Do you see?"

Not really, but he checked again until he found some of the brighter stars that might have been a figure if a toddler had drawn it, with something attached to hands that didn't exist. "I think I found it."

"They've measured that constellation as something like two hundred million light-years away." Her lips came closer to his ear. "Two hundred million! Think of how fast light moves. Of how far it must reach in an entire year. Of how vast that distance truly is..." She sighed, and he convulsed in a delicious shudder as her breath feathered over the downy hairs on the back of his neck as her voice lowered to reverential tones. "Have you ever felt so insignificant? So small and yet so miraculous?"

Turning his head toward her voice, Eli found her huddled beside him, patiently waiting her turn.

The answer to her question was *hell no*. So he didn't speak it.

He felt large and hard and very fucking significant right now. Vital. Alive. Infused with whatever mysterious force hurled those chunks of fire across the sky, and burning just as hot.

Honeysuckle and herbs. Skin smooth as porcelain, even this close. Soft eyes. Warm, sweet breath from plump peach lips. The kind of lips that would look perfect stretched around his—

"Here." He straightened and backed away from the telescope. "It's your meteor shower. You can watch it now."

Her eyes crinkled with a pleased smile as she took his place, bending over the telescope in a position that didn't help his predicament in the slightest.

"It's not my meteor shower, it's Andromeda's."

"Who?"

"Andromeda. The Chained Lady." She fiddled with a knob, and he saw the edge of the telescope grow in length.

Which reminded him of his own state of affairs.

"In Greek mythology, Andromeda was a princess of Ethiopia," Rosaline continued, blithely unaware of his present state of abject arousal. "Her mother, Cassiopeia, told everyone she was more beautiful than the Nereids, so Poseidon, the sea god, punished the entire kingdom and demanded sacrifice. The people chained Andromeda to the rocks to sacrifice her to a sea monster, but Perseus saved her life and married her, making her his queen."

He grunted out a response and turned to retreat to the railing, curling his fingers around it until the knuckles pressed white against the scarred or broken skin. He stayed like that for a moment, willing his libido under control. Doing his best not to wonder if his hands would span her entire waist. If her hair was as silky as it looked. If—

"Mr. Wolfe?"

"Hmm?"

"Do you think we should kiss?"

The question stopped his heart for two full beats before he could whirl back around to face her.

She'd abandoned the telescope to stand before him, her hands clasped primly in front of her.

Damned if she didn't look like a virgin…

Damned if he didn't find that alluring as all get out.

Damned…was what he was for wanting like hell to corrupt her.

"I don't think it's a good idea," he finally replied, calculating how quickly he could get to the door before she pressed the point.

"Do you...not want to kiss me?"

"No!" He held up his hand. "I mean yes. Of course I do. I just..."

"Have you not done much kissing?" she queried.

He scratched that place behind his ear, again. The one that tingled when he was unnerved. "Can't say as I have..."

"Me either." She stepped forward with a shy, encouraging smile. "None, in fact. Perhaps it's best we're both new at...relations between—"

"Oh, I've had *plenty* of relations," he blurted before he could think better of it. "Just the kind I have don't generally include much in the way of kissing and whatnot."

A frown creased her brow and pouted out her lower lip in a way that made him want to nibble the expression away.

Fucking hell, he was in so much trouble.

"Why not?" she asked.

Well, he'd been honest thus far...might as well keep it on the straight and narrow. "Because men like me don't have time for dawdling. I usually employ women for—for that kind of thing, or take up an offer from a lonely widow or the like. My relations, as you call them, are often just a transaction. More scratching an itch than any kind of kissing situation."

Her nose wrinkled, but she seemed more puzzled than distressed by his answer. "Why aren't kisses part of the transaction?"

He plunged his fingers into his hair, scraping his scalp. "Hell. I don't know. Because kissing is different, I guess. It's—more affectionate than sex. It's bonding, you could call it."

"I see." She pursed her lips together, pondering his words before coming to a conclusion. "If we're to be married to each other, doesn't it make sense that we should bond physically?"

Wait. Was she saying she wanted to fuck? "Miss Goode... Didn't Morley tell you this would be a marriage in name only?"

"He mentioned the possibility. But my wedded siblings so obviously enjoy their spouses. Even Pru and Morley had to marry under terrible circumstances, and they're mad for each other now." The hands in front of her seemed to clench tighter, though she remained outwardly serene. "I know we've no time for courtship, per se, but don't you think a marriage of convenience would make you awfully lonely over the years?"

"I don't mind lonely." Lonely was safe. Lonely was freedom. Lonely...was all he knew.

"Oh." She blinked rapidly, her shoulders deflating as a rash of color crawled from beneath her collar. "Oh. I see." Turning, she picked up the pencil from where it rested in the open spine of the logbook. Dropped it. Retrieved it. "I-I understand now. I suppose I didn't realize—that is..." Closing the logbook, she set the pencil down beside it. "I thought the marriage in name only was for my benefit, rather than yours," she told the far wall.

Aw hell, he'd made her feel rejected.

"It was," Eli rushed. "It *is*. Morley and I thought since such unfortunate and unforeseen circumstances forced us into this—"

"No. Yes. You needn't explain." She gathered up a shawl from the table next to the logbook, and didn't seem to notice when her abandoned pencil rolled off the edge and clattered to the floor. "It is my fault we find ourselves in this...unfortunate circumstance." Visibly battling for her composure, she wrapped the shawl around her shoulders. "I was out of line just now, Mr. Wolfe. I hope you'll forgive—erm—I should go."

Clutching the shawl to herself like a shield, she ducked

her head and scurried forward, obviously intending to rush past him before he saw any tears fall.

Before he made the conscious decision to do so, Eli reached out and clamped his hand around her upper arm. "Wait."

"Please," she whispered on a suspicious hitch of breath. "I really should—"

He searched a head empty of blood for something to say. "Look. This doesn't have anything to do with you."

"Oh God." She lifted both hands to her mouth. "You're in love with another woman and I ruined it for you both."

"That's not it."

She eyed him carefully, dare he say, hopefully. "Another…man, then?"

"No!" He put his hands up against any more guesses. "*No*," he repeated. "It's just that—I mean— Aw hell, I don't know what I mean." Plunging fingers through his hair he tugged in frustration as he paced away from the dais and returned to it in several swift strides before squaring his shoulders and pinning her with a hard stare.

"Goddammit, look at me, Rosaline." He opened his arms and presented himself for inspection. "I'm a man more comfortable with a pickaxe in his hand than a teacup. I'm a heavy-fisted juggernaut with more scars than sense and prone to more cussing than culture. And you?" He tossed a gesture at her entire person, which seemed smaller and more vulnerable than ever.

"You're just a little bitty thing with those doe eyes that take up most of your face. You're young and fresh and innocent and I'm not only old enough to be your father, but I'm just about used up by hunger and ambition and… Christ. I just—I don't know, I feel like kissing you makes me some kind of middle-aged pervert. Wanting you is like a golem wanting a goddess."

At this point, Eli didn't know what kind of fool words were spewing from his mouth, they just flowed in a tirade of frustration, lust, and a foreign need to keep the dampness clumping her lashes together from spilling down her blush-stained cheeks.

"It's damned strange," he lamented. "I'm not a man who is clumsy around women...but *you*. You come in here looking like a schoolboy's wicked fantasy and show me these stars—meteors—whatever they are. Mesmerize me with mythology and beggared if you don't spin my axis until I don't know which way is up or—"

He didn't see her move until she was in his arms.

Or he was in hers.

After a breath it didn't matter, because her sleek, slender body pressed against his and she was clinging to his shoulders as if letting go would send her tumbling down a mine shaft.

In the past, such a move had been followed by a crash of mouths. The ripping of clothing. Passionate, violent, loud fucking.

Sure, kissing might be involved, mostly on places other than the mouth.

But Rosaline...in the twenty-four hours since they'd met, she'd failed to do anything he expected. He'd be a fool to imagine anything else now.

She lifted onto the tips of her toes, her hands reaching up to cup his face and drag it down toward her. Eyes closed, mouth artlessly seeking, she held him by the jaw and planted what he could only identify as a gentle but determined kiss square on his mouth.

It lasted a stunned second, maybe two, before she pulled back and searched his face, eyes touching everywhere. Lips parted. His jaw still a prisoner of her palms.

Eli stared down at her, rocked in a way he'd never been before. Overwhelmed by her scent. By the surprising strength of her grip and the confounding way in which someone so physically different from him in every way seemed to conform to him as if she'd been crafted to do so.

"Oh my," she said, as if something important had been decided.

"Oh no," he groaned as his head lowered to capture her mouth again. The heat that at once surged through him was followed by a cold, hollow ache. One that'd been mined in the depths of the earth so long ago, a void he carried around with him that refused to be filled no matter what wealth he acquired.

She was a dainty morsel of pleasure. An epicurean delicacy placed before a wolf used to tearing into flesh with his teeth and claws. He hardly knew what to do with a woman like this.

As his thoughts scattered like a bag of marbles on a concrete floor, his body reacted to her kiss as if it'd been waiting for one like this since kissing had been invented. With a skill he'd forgotten he possessed, he swept his lips over hers in deep, drugging passes before teasing the seam of her delectable mouth with his tongue.

Pleasure and pain mingled within him. She was like a storm approaching a dying man. First, he would lap at the rain, open his mouth and drink until his thirst was quenched and his life restored.

But the winds would come, and the lightning would drive him back. The thunder would tear at the skies. The clouds would hide her precious stars.

That was the thing about storms. They were beautiful...until you were swept away in their wake.

The small, wet tip of her tongue met his in a shy greeting.

And all the dark thoughts he harbored dissipated in a flood of pure lust. He tried to keep the kiss gentle. He really did. A lifetime of deprivation did not create a patient man. When he indulged, it was with a gluttonous greed.

He'd always fucked like he fed, with the frenzy of a man who wasn't certain of his next meal.

And he didn't stop until they were both too exhausted to come again.

But this... This was new.

Their kiss turned thick, like golden honey warmed by the sun. Long and languid and unbearably sweet. There was nowhere to go from here. Not tonight. Nothing else needed doing but this.

He tasted her in slick, slow swipes as his mind rushed to commit every sensation to memory.

So if she was taken from him, he could remember this in the lonely dark.

His arms unclenched from around her, his hands finding the fall of silken hair down her back, learning the thick, yet fine texture of it. Charting the shape of her spine, her waist. Finding that his hands did, indeed, nearly span the circumference of it.

A small sound broke from her throat, and it vibrated between them, shivering through his bones and echoing in the chamber of his heart.

Never in his life had he been so consumed by a kiss. Never had a hundred heartbeats gone by without him noticing anything but the pleasure of the moments. Never had desire thundered through him with such strength, it shook him to the foundations of everything that made him a man.

A lightning strike of primal demand forked through him, bringing every single nerve ending alive with electric longing. With the unslakable desire that so often drove him to the brink of sanity.

All he could think about was how she would look impaled by his cock.

He tore his lips from hers with a growl, unable to disengage from the featherlight weight of her sagging against him. "Goddamn but you're dainty," he moaned the reminder to himself. "So easy to break."

Her eyes were luminous, her flesh high with color and her lips swollen and abraded by his evening's growth of whiskers. "I don't think you'll break me," she whispered.

That proved how little she knew him.

Lifting a hand, he cupped her face, stroking the downy place her cheekbone melted into her hairline. "I'll try not to, darlin'."

What did a good man do with a wife like this? How did he keep someone so fragile and frail safe from everything in this world that would, in fact, do its best to break her?

How did he keep these deviant thoughts and primitive desires from staining her sweet, civilized soul?

Disentangling himself from her arms, he turned away and adjusted himself before he opened the door. "You should go, Miss Goode. It still isn't proper for you to be here so late."

She gazed at him for a quiet moment, her eyes bewildered and uncomprehending. Clearing the fog with several rapid blinks, she tasted her lips with a smile he knew she didn't realize was full of sex and satisfaction.

Fuck. She had to go. She had to go now.

She floated toward the door as if her feet didn't touch the ground, stopping to press her hand to his forearm in a fond gesture. "Goodnight, Mr. Wolfe," she bade in a voice several octaves huskier than the usual trill. "I-I will look forward to seeing you soon."

She wouldn't. Because the next time he saw her this tenuous tether he'd clamped to his self-control would snap.

Distance was the only think that'd keep him sane until then.

Closing the door against her, he let his shoulders sag and dragged a scratchy palm over his face. Obsession. Addiction. His mother had been prone to it. So many men in his life drowned in desire for something that tore them away from what mattered.

Eli had never understood it until now.

She was just such a distraction. A complication he sure as fuck didn't need.

One he wanted too much.

He had to stay away from her. At least until the wedding. Once they had that disaster done, he'd figure out where to put her. Wherever she wanted to be, of course. With whatever she wanted.

So long as what she wanted wasn't his time or his heart.

Because he had neither to give.

CHAPTER 6

Five men.

Rosaline could count the males with whom she'd had a relationship—or an entire conversation—on one hand.

Her indifferent father. Her damaged brother. Her vicious uncle. Doddering old Doctor Pritchard back in Hampshire. And the endlessly decent Sir Carlton. She'd three more brothers-in-law, but Titus Conleith was a new father and busy preeminent surgeon, and the other two had been abroad practically since they'd been introduced. This didn't leave them very much time to become closely acquainted.

Five men.

And now...she had a husband.

A husband she couldn't stop staring at.

A husband she'd barely had a glimpse of in two weeks.

A husband who refused to spare her more than a passing glance the entirety of their wedding day.

After a profoundly mediocre ceremony sealed with a perfunctory kiss on the corner of her mouth, Mr. Wolfe—Eli—had abandoned her to preparations for the ball they were throwing in lieu of a honeymoon.

Another wedding was to be had not a month hereafter, and it was explained that Elijah and Rosaline Wolfe would not disembark until the young Baron, Emmett, and his bride, Lucy, were well on their way to wedded bliss.

Rather than enjoying one of the few balls she'd been invited to attend, one that had been thrown in her own honor, Rosaline retreated to a shadowy nook above the grand staircase at the first opportunity to indulge in a bit of panic and self-pity.

She gazed down through the ornate banner to the resplendent scene below. From her vantage, she could only see the swirling hems of glittering gowns as they waltzed across a dance floor she'd not been invited to.

Her husband didn't dance, apparently.

The fortnight since she'd enjoyed her first kiss was now a haze of chaos. Her fiancé didn't visit but once, and that was to commiserate with Morley, who explained that Eli was seeing to some business interests before their wedding.

Though she'd been disappointed, Rosaline had believed Morley.

She'd had to.

Because the alternative was that with one kiss, he'd changed his mind about the entire thing. Or, with one kiss, the pleasant evening they'd spent had been wiped from his mind, replaced with revulsion.

Could she have done it wrong, the kissing?

To her, it'd felt so extraordinarily right. In fact, after his impassioned tirade, admitting he found her desirable, she'd abandoned a very instinctual fear of intimacy of any kind, and leapt into the kiss with all of herself.

Perhaps *he'd* wanted to be the one in control of the kiss. Maybe he'd disliked that she used her tongue in the same fashion he had done.

That she'd taken a taste for herself.

Men, as she understood it, liked it when women

were submissive, silent, and still. She'd been neither during their interlude, becoming this unrecognizable creature of sensation driven by a heady instinct born of need.

It occurred to her that *this* was why people in his realm *didn't* kiss. Because of how distracting it was. Indeed, she'd thought of little else since.

At night, she'd lie in bed and imagine that the taste of him still lingered on her lips. Warm skin spiced with all things masculine and mysterious.

There in the dark, she'd dream his hands were on her again, large and strong and careful. She'd conjure the press of his lips to her mind, running her fingers along her mouth in a pale attempt to capture the same sensation.

In her heart, she secretly wished he did the same. Perhaps not so frivolously as she, as he was a stern sort of man without the leisure of romantic idealism. But she hoped he thought of her in a few idle moments of his busy days and smiled. That he looked forward to their next kiss. And more.

She looked across the way from her bedroom window often at night, wondering which chamber in Hespera House was his.

Which one would be hers?

A fortnight ago, Rosaline had been devastated to learn that she'd have to marry.

But their kiss had given her hope. Not only the kiss, but the reverent gasp he made when he watched the stars. The open curiosity he showed when she spoke of things that excited and inspired her.

She'd left Hespera House *liking* her husband-to-be.

It was why she'd expended so much effort for the wedding.

Her hopelessly straight hair had been in curling wraps for two nights, and she'd even allowed Emmett to splurge on one of the most heavenly wedding dresses she could imagine.

Nora had suggested she wear the family jewels and Baroness tiara for the occasion.

When Rosaline had looked in the mirror right before the ceremony, she hadn't recognized herself. Eyes bright with a bit of hope. With anticipation. A neckline that swooped just below her shoulders and skimmed the tops of her breasts in a way that made her look as if she *had* any breasts to speak of.

She'd felt like a princess. Like a woman a wealthy man like Elijah Wolfe would be pleased to see as his approaching bride.

Except, he hadn't been.

Once she appeared on Emmett's arm to advance up the aisle, Eli had dashed a swift glance at her, then affixed his gaze somewhere above her head as his expression shifted from grim to grave.

Rosaline had a lifetime of hiding her emotions from a man who didn't want to see them, but it was all she could do to stop a disappointed tear from escaping.

In fact, escape was all she'd sought since. A quiet place to grieve her dashed hopes and muster up the courage to face him.

To face him every day until death did they part.

Unless he planned on stashing her away somewhere he wouldn't be bothered by her.

Just like her father had done to her mother.

Her sallow, bitter, cruel mother who died early of nothing more than disappointment and distemper, leaving her children to the mercy of Uncle Reginald.

Worrying at the inside of her cheek with her teeth, Rosaline blinked when an emerald-green skirt and a cup of punch appeared in front of her.

Emmaline, her only full-blooded elder sister, always had a knack for finding her when others seemed perfectly content to allow her to disappear. "I added a bit of spice to it."

Spice was her secret word for spirits.

Scanning the ballroom with her Baltic blue eyes, Emmaline scratched at the matching dress that set her copper hair aflame. "Do we *know* any of these bloody people?"

"*Emma*," Rosaline admonished in a loud whisper, though there was no real heat in it. "Someone will hear you."

She waved Rosaline's worry away with a hand she'd relieved of a glove before pinning her with a pensive examination. "Did something happen? You're not quite the cheerful woman you were this morning."

Cursing Emma's observant nature, Rosaline smoothed her hand over the curls that were quickly becoming as limp as she felt. How did she share the strange and fickle emotions swirling inside of her? How did she burden someone who cared about her in all this helplessness she battled?

"I'm just…a bit overstimulated," she lied, painting on a placating smile.

Emma threaded their arms together, careful of the fine dress and the artfully arranged hair and veil. "You made the most beautiful bride I've ever seen," she sighed, kissing Rosaline on the cheek. "And your groom isn't difficult to look at either."

No. No he wasn't.

If Rosaline had been asked to remember a word of the ceremony, she'd have failed miserably. Because, even though her husband hadn't been impressed with her, *she'd* almost lost her wits at the sight of him.

They called him Midas, but if Rosaline were to give him a mythological assignation, it would be none other than Hades himself.

Not a being of light, but a dark-haired, flinty-eyed

God. One who'd crafted a kingdom beneath the earth and ripped gold from stones and ore. His features were a perfect canvas for the stark and brutal bones beneath them.

Stealing covert glances during the ceremony had forced her to notice only one defining feature at a time. The grooves etched in the corners of his eyes. The sparse threads of silver anointing the dark hair at his temple. The strong cut of his jaw that wanted a shave by three in the afternoon. The lackadaisical arrangement of his limbs, loose and lethal when so many of her countrymen were taught to stand with regimental posture.

He presented the image of a predator at rest. A wolf in the woods surveying his territory as, though he was in a foreign country, it seemed that any land he stood upon was claimed by him.

That it would be easier to move a mountain than the man.

The constant challenge in his eyes invited anyone to try.

Rosaline had yearned to examine his rough, scarred hand as she'd slid on the ring with trembling fingers. The gold band had been simple and wide, cold and hard to the touch.

Like him.

As she understood it, he was a being of the desert, a man used to unthinkable heat and a relentless sun. How did he fare in their damp, chilly land?

She'd given his chilled hand a squeeze between the two of her own after sliding the ring into place, hoping to impart some of her warmth.

Without reciprocation, or even acknowledgment, he'd extracted his hand from hers, his fingers closing into tight fists.

"Why are you hiding here?" Emma asked with gentle solemnity settling onto the stair beside her. "Is this not a happy day?"

Swallowing the sand in her throat, Rosaline studied her own ring, also gold, though a few diamonds winked from where they were inlayed into the band like little captured stars. "I was hoping for a happy match, despite the circumstances, but I don't think Mr. Wolfe is at all pleased to be called my husband."

Emma's expression darkened as much as her gingery complexion would allow. "If he's unhappy with you, Ros, he's a fool."

"I don't know..." Plucking at a stray thread on her sleeve, she fought back emotion with all the fervency of a besieged stronghold.

Once the walls collapsed, there'd be nothing to protect what was inside. Her soft, vulnerable underbelly so often exposed to bruising blows and crushing cruelty.

"Emma, he thinks of me as little more than a child. He's used to bold American women. Ones who know how to...to entice men. I'm too fragile for him. He says he's afraid to break me, but I'm terrified of the moment when he finds out I'm already broken."

"Hush, you." Emma squeezed her close. "You mustn't talk like that. You're not broken, darling, you're simply uncompleted. You're a young woman who has yet to finish becoming who she was meant to be. Certainly, you can't be broken before you're even made."

Filled to the brim with gratitude, Rosaline leaned into her sister's embrace, resting her head on her shoulder. "You're so kind, but—"

Emma's hand clamped over her mouth as the click of several finely cobbled heels on the parquet floors filtered up through the staircase banister.

Another pair of women, or perhaps a trio, had paused on the floor beneath the dark landing on which the Goode sisters perched, to indulge in a bit of gossip.

"...size of his hands is positively obscene," one said

under her breath. "They were as callused as my land-keeper's."

"Aren't you and your land-keeper *lovers*?" Another lady added syrup to her sneer to make it more palatable, Rosaline supposed.

"Only because I hadn't met Mr. Elijah Wolfe yet," said the first before a rip of fabric announced that she'd opened her fan. "In my experience, men who look like that fornicate like animals. They'll shape you into the most vexing positions and pound you past all semblance of sanity."

A third companion simpered. "When have you ever come into contact with a man like that? God doesn't make his ilk in our Empire."

"Oh, he sends us a few, though one does have to search carefully, and often in Scotland."

"I wonder if he's as ruthless in bed as he is in business," the second woman sighed. "I worry for the wife."

"She's an odd little mouse, isn't she? They seem so ill matched. It appears to me a marriage of convenience, or perhaps of circumstance."

"Which means he'll be in the market for a mistress..."

The atmosphere veritably vibrated with excitement as Rosaline's stomach seized and twisted so violently, she pressed a hand to her mouth, afraid to be sick.

Emma surged to her feet, fists curled into balls of wrath. "I'm going to put a stop to this."

"Don't." Rosaline seized her hand and pulled, leveraging her help to stand. "Don't make a scene. It's just a bit of gossip."

She wanted to feel as tranquil about it as she conveyed, but both her body and her mind were dizzy with a dervish of emotions and anxieties.

Though she'd known her husband all of a dozen days, and had interacted with him seldom in that time, the thought of him taking a mistress was untenable.

Especially *them.* Those women who had already guessed she was too much a mouse to please him.

Was it an opinion her husband shared?

"Rosaline…" Emma stepped down a stair and faced her, bringing them eye level as she was several inches taller and more regal. "Has anyone discussed the wedding night with you?"

"It's generally thought among our family that this will be a marriage in name only."

Emma's steady eyes searched her own. "Is that what you truly want?"

Gulping, Rosaline shook her head. "I want what our sisters have. Affection, passion…but I don't think Mr. Wolfe is the kind of man who—"

"Hang what kind of man he is," Emma said with a quiet but fervent passion. "You are one of the loveliest women on this green earth. It was why Uncle Reginald hid you from everyone. It was why he was critical and malicious toward you over the rest of us, because he didn't want you to realize your worth. Rosaline, he was going to sell you to a wealthy bidder to marry, and your revenge is that you ended up with one of the wealthiest men in the world, and he doesn't get a penny."

That brought a faint smile to Rosaline's stiff features. She had more reason to hate Uncle Reginald than even her siblings realized.

"I kissed Mr. Wolfe," she confided. "And he seemed to enjoy it. But then he…well, he hasn't spoken to me since."

"Then speak to *him*, Ros," Emma said with an eye roll. "Make him take notice. We women are expected to spend all our lives waiting for a man to tell us what to do next. To wait and be available at his pleasure. Well, I know I wasn't born with male parts, but this is me giving you permission to stop hiding up high where no one can see you. Go to your husband. Let him look at you. He won't be able to help but be impressed. Enamored, I dare say."

"He hasn't looked at me all day," Rosaline lamented.

Emma regarded her as if she'd sprouted horns. "What nonsense are you talking? Granted, he's been attempting to remain furtive, but when he looks at you, Rosaline, even my breath catches in my throat. I've seen starving men staring at a tenderloin with less longing."

Rosaline's eyes widened. "Truly?"

"Stop being a ninny and *go*," Emma urged with the sort of fond impatience only elder sisters seemed to employ.

Rosaline descended the stairs on unsteady feet, wishing she'd not insisted upon taller heels to make her seem less comically short beside her husband. The floor seemed extra slippery. The ground beneath her threatened to fall away at any moment.

Both literally and figuratively.

She paused in the entry to the ballroom to search for Eli, feeling a hundred or so sets of eyes upon her as well as a thousand pinpricks of trepidation.

There.

He was so easy to find, standing both taller and wider than most men.

As his back was to her, she took a moment to gaze at him. To watch the light streaming through the windows glance off the tamed mane of his dark hair. To appreciate the lines of him, breadth and depth and length all scrupulously tethered by toughened sinew and unimaginable strength.

His skin weathered by the elements and painted by even brief encounters with the uncompromising Nevada sun, he was positively swarthy, surrounded by her famously pallid countrymen.

A circle of gentlemen had gathered around him, their heads pressed close as they discussed something so intently, she was loath to interrupt.

"Congratulations again, dear sister," Emmett said,

kissing her cheek. "You make the most ravishing bride. Have you seen Emma?"

"Don't you mean Lucy?"

His smile turned to ash, though he fought to cover it most valiantly. "I've danced with her thrice, now. Any more would be obscene."

With a sympathetic squeeze of his arm, Rosaline directed him to the stairs and drifted through the crowd of strangers. Some added their well wishes, and others simply stared as if she were a Hydra sprouting more heads than was proper.

It didn't matter.

They didn't matter. She knew so many of them wished to be attached to her husband's fortune. And now she realized just how fervently many of them would wish to share his bed, as well.

As she approached Eli from behind, several of the men redirected their appreciative gazes down toward her rather than on the debate her husband was immersed in.

His broad back was tense, his voice guttural and gravely as he gestured to the scowling, portly man across from him. "The salient point here is that tungsten is the strongest of *any* natural metal, and is used to alloy steel to make it stronger. American architects and construction giants are ravenous for it as they race to build structures as tall as the Tower of Babel itself. More stories than you can possibly imagine. You've no idea what a treasure that cache in Devon truly is, Mr. Crompton, but I'm telling you now—"

"That's *Lord* Crompton to you, young man." The Baron shook his jowls in outrage.

"Maybe to your nationals, but I claim no man as lord." Eli stated this without gravitas or ire, but simple fact. "Regardless, what I was saying—"

"The cheek of this upstart colonial!" Lord Crompton's pate, visible beneath his dearth of sparse silver hair, darkened from red to purple. "How *dare* you presume to tell me what to accept into my own refineries. You've not an ounce of legal bearing and certainly no breeding or family connections to speak of. Were I a younger man, I'd teach you some bloody respect. I've been in this business for five and twenty years! You were scarcely out of the nursery."

"I was picking iron out of stone with my own bare hands by then." Dark color also climbed from beneath her husband's collar, belying his controlled intonation. "And I invite you all to tell me who has more credibility, a man who has amassed the holdings and fortune I have in the course of a single decade, or a man who's been in the trade twice as long, and is barely solvent enough to keep his machinery in working order or his employees paid decent wages. I don't give a dusty fuck if you're an aristocrat, an autocrat, or a bureaucrat, if you want my respect you have to earn it first."

Even Rosaline joined in the gasp at Eli's frank and grievous assessment.

He didn't know. He didn't realize that he'd levered what was possibly the two most heinous insults at the man in the space of a handful of sentences. One didn't mention personal finances in public and one *certainly* didn't make light of another man's title.

Ever.

Crompton looked as if his head might pop like a grape beneath the pressure of his fury. When he spoke, droplets of froth and spittle spewed from his lips. "Irrespective of what you Americans have in undeserved resources, you've yet to learn that dignity and nobility cannot be bought. And neither can my refineries! I'll consign them to hell before I see them sullied by your tungsten, you insufferable—"

Rosaline stepped around her husband, inserting herself into the circle of perhaps a dozen men before she could think better of it. She hated the attention of so many, and yet she felt as if it were this, or a real-life gunfight in the streets at high noon. Er, in this case, half past five.

That, or the Baron would suffer an apoplexy on her wedding day.

"Lord Crompton," she greeted with a demure curtsy. "I've been meaning to thank you for your attendance here. I have made the acquaintance of your handsome, spirited grandson who is playing with a litter of kittens in the parlor. How proud you must be of him."

"Miss Rosaline," he sputtered, blinking a few times before returning to glare above her crown where Eli was, no doubt, returning the expression in kind. "I've come because your late father was a friend and equal in business *and* dignity, but I'm uncertain whether to express my felicitations or my condolences on this occasion."

Gulping down her nerves, she reached back for Eli's arm without looking, relieved when he stepped abreast of her to give it.

The muscle beneath his fine suit may as well have been crafted from the alloy they'd just been discussing, hard and unyielding as it was beneath her fingers.

There was violence in this man. Primal and predatory, it shimmered in the air around him, so foreign in such refined environs.

"You'll have to excuse my husband, Lord Crompton," she said in a remarkably clear voice for how deeply she trembled. "He's never been informed that our titles are very much like that of elected officials in his own country, a designation of rank, respect, and propriety. Much like my new delineation as Mrs. Wolfe rather than Miss Rosaline."

It took two very obvious swallows fraught with an expectant silence from all the men for the Baron to contain himself enough to reply. "You'll forgive my breach of manners, Mrs. Wolfe, and I will consider the same courtesy for your husband."

"Nothing to forgive, my lord." She pasted on her most winsome smile, regardless of the waves of malevolence rolling from her husband's incomprehensively large shoulders. "Likewise, my darling husband doesn't realize how progressive men like you and my father were in an ancient society such as ours. When it became evident that landowners were losing fortunes, you turned to trade to keep up with the times, despite the naysayers amongst your peers."

The Baron's features relaxed as more people began to pause and take notice of the conversation. "Your husband does not possess your depth of perspective, my lady, he is too busy chasing fabled treasures and buying up land and resources that he should have no claim to."

Stepping forward before her husband could reply, she placed a placating hand on one of the arms Lord Crompton had crossed over his chest. "I read something recently that stuck with me. Let me see, how does it go? 'A man who has a hundred thousand pounds cannot understand a man who has twenty. Just as a man who has twenty years cannot understand a man who has one hundred.' I should like to venture that a man who has no king cannot understand a one who has been blessed with royal favor. And a man who was born into the privilege and nobility of Her Majesty's court cannot understand one who is ungoverned by the same...constructs. And so, in my opinion, true treasure is perspective, is it not?"

"You are wise beyond your years, my girl." Crompton patted her hand.

"It's my experience, my lord, that perspective is gained through civil discourse, and I realize you've not been the recipient of civility today, but perhaps you and Mr. Wolfe might meet at a more appropriate time? Then you may discuss how wealthy building an empire of steel and—

tungsten, was it?—might make you both if you could set cultural differences aside."

A few of the men muttered their assent, and she could feel others holding their collective breaths as their eyes affixed to the man at her side.

His ribs expanded, pressing into her arm as he took a deep breath, and Rosaline finally ventured a look up at him.

Stone-faced and enigmatic as ever, he made the crowd wait until his lungs had slowly emptied to say, "I would welcome such a discussion…Lord Crompton."

The acquiescence didn't go unnoticed, and many of those gathered visibly relaxed.

For his part, Crompton stepped forward and took her hand, bowing over it. "You are certainly one of his more valuable acquisitions, Mrs. Wolfe. I hope he recognizes that."

Though she flinched at the word acquisition…she added her hope to that of Crompton's, as he straightened and nodded to her husband.

"I shall have my secretary contact yours to schedule further discussion," he said stiffly. "Perhaps it would behoove you to bring your new bride." With that, he waddled away, his round belly proceeding him by several inches.

Rosaline wanted to sag with relief, but a new dawning anxiety wouldn't allow it.

The arm beneath hers remained rigid as steel as he did an abrupt turn, forcing her to step quickly in order to keep up.

"If you'll excuse us, gentlemen," she rushed as Eli strode toward the balcony on the other side of the sideboard, leaving her no choice but to let him go or be dragged along.

Trotting to keep up with him, she nearly crashed into his back when he stopped abruptly to swipe a glass of champagne from the refreshment table and finish it in one gulp before draining another in two.

That accomplished, he marched out the balcony doors and into an afternoon swiftly fading into evening. His pace never faltered until he reached the balcony railing and gripped it with both hands, eyes affixed to the London skyline painted the same dark tone against the vanishing sun.

Rosaline released his arm to allow him space to take the air as deeply and desperately as he'd downed the champagne. His breath slowed after a moment, and he even covered a mild, closed-mouth burp as the champagne bubbles executed their escape.

Eventually, he let out a deep breath through his nose, closing his eyes as if asking God why he'd cursed him with such cruel misfortune.

"Please don't be cross," she implored. "I didn't intend to—"

"The pretentious ass is right, you know." He squinted in the direction of the dying light, his jaw working as if he chewed on something bitter. "You might have just saved me a mountain of work and even more money."

Rosaline didn't understand. His dark tone didn't match his expression in the least. "And…that is a good thing, yes?"

He leveled her a sidelong look. "In what world would it be a bad thing?"

"Well, you seem as if you were just forced to chew glass and then drink the juice of lemons."

He barked out a harsh, caustic sound that might have been a laugh. "My entire life, men like that have tried to crush me beneath their boot heel. They compete for my money, all the while trying to remind me that without it, I'd be nothing more than a stain they could wipe from the bottom of their shoe. I'd give my left—er—eye to throw them down the pit I cut my teeth in and watch them blister their soft hands in order to dig out. Hell, I'd chew glass just to spit blood in their faces." To elucidate his point, he spat over the railing as if ridding himself of a foul taste.

Impulsively, Rosaline stepped beside him and did the same, her own imitation of his curt spit falling pathetically short of the masculine gravitas his had conveyed.

"I understand how you feel," she murmured, instantly regretting that she'd spoken her innermost thoughts out loud.

Looking up, she found him watching her with a peculiar expression, as if truly seeing her for the first time. "Yeah... Yeah, I bet you do," he said, his voice softening to a low rumble.

His gaze didn't rest upon her for long, and they stood there at the balcony in a strangely companionable silence, their breaths synchronizing as they studied the broken horizon.

This man. *Her husband.* He never ceased to surprise her. When she'd expected him to take out his ire upon her, to punish her for stepping in front of him in an altercation, to be furious that she'd admitted his ignorance to an entire crowd of men, he'd not even mentioned it.

In fact, his words had almost sounded like gratitude.

"I need this fucking day to be over," he rumbled as if to himself.

This day. Their wedding day.

Smothering a flicker of hurt, Rosaline smoothed a hand down her bodice, stopping to fidget with one of the sparkling beads adorning the waistline. "I've been thinking," she ventured. "I realize this isn't the marriage either of us pictured for ourselves. But perhaps you and I could attempt something like you and Lord Crompton will. A summit of sorts, and you could convey your stipulations or requirements of me. If I had more of an idea what you desire—of what sort of woman appeals to your tastes... If

I knew what I could do or learn to make you more...attracted."

"Attracted?" He said every syllable of the word as if he'd never heard it before, staring at her like she'd gone quite suddenly mad. "What tomfuckery are you talking, woman?"

Squirming beneath the intensity of his confounded regard, she fervently wished she'd said nothing. "The other night..." She made a gesture that she hoped would lead him to the memory of their kiss without having to say it plainly. "I must have insulted you, repulsed you, even, and I realize I'd never—kissed anyone before. I wasn't certain what to do with my tongue and I was hoping with a bit of practice I might improve and—"

"Jesus Josephat Christ," he growled, seizing her arm and propelling her toward the far left of the balcony, out of eyesight and earshot of any guests. "There's no possible way you thought I was disgusted by that kiss," he hissed rather aggressively, in her opinion. "Couldn't you tell by how—was it not physically obvious what that did to me?"

Wrinkling her forehead, she shrugged her lack of understanding. "I thought we might have established a rapport, if not a fondness for each other. But you haven't so much as acknowledged my existence since then. Nor have we spoken since." A wave of emotion threatened to erupt from her, and she swallowed convulsively so as not to humiliate herself further.

He slapped the brick with the flat of his hand and then leaned on it, using his other hand to dig at his eyeballs in acute frustration. "This right here is why I shouldn't have a wife. I've no idea how to explain this shit to you."

The ache of tears turned into a sting, welling so quickly into her eyes she choked down a sob with what little remained of her strength. "Be honest with me. I can take it. What did I do wrong?"

"Wrong?" he thundered before pressing his lips in a

hard line and checking over his shoulder for eavesdroppers. "No, goddammit, how could you not tell that I was one more moan away from making a woman out of you right there on the table? I was little better than a predator with a hard pecker, and I was liable to toss your schoolmarm skirt over your pretty head and plow right into you. That would have made me the worst sort of monster. So, I removed all temptation because I had all this shit to do, and I can't very well *think* if I'm constantly faced with what I want the most."

Agape, Rosaline stared up at his scowl, her heart lifting as if someone had forgotten to tie it down. "The most?" she echoed in disbelief.

He made a gesture of his own incredulity. "Oh, don't go acting like you don't know you're the prettiest girl in the room. That people don't see my ornery, uncivilized, work-weathered hide and pity you for having to put up with me until I die."

Jaw still slack, Rosaline shook her head in abject rejection of his every word. "Not two minutes ago, I listened to three women plan to compete for the position of your mistress once you've thrown me over."

His brows slammed together. "Say what, now?"

"They gave all sorts of salacious speculations regarding how you would treat them. How rough you would be with them. I believe the word they used was...pounding."

A sound between a gasp, a cough, and a chuckle depressed his ribs as he came to stand directly over her. Some of the tension in his shoulders abated, and his hard features softened as his fingers hovered somewhere below her jaw and above her shoulder, as if unsure of where to land. "I'm not the kind of man to break our vows unless you release me from them, you understand?"

She nodded, mollified. "That's why you wanted the

day to be over, because you think these people are judging you?"

"I know they are, but I don't give a dusty fuck about that."

"Then why—"

"Because I don't like having to talk to all these people I don't know. And the people I do know are men like Crompton who want to discuss business at my wedding without discussing money and I can't stand all these godforsaken rules I keep breaking before I learn them. On top of that, everyone keeps asking me why I haven't waltzed with you."

Before she thought better of it, she asked, "Why haven't you waltzed with me?"

"Because I never did such a thing my whole life, I'm not about to start now, what with you looking so expensive and wearing heels high enough to snap your ankle if I trip you. I'd hang myself with this fucking awful tie before I'd let that happen."

Rosaline knew she shouldn't be smiling, but she couldn't seem to wipe the pleasure from her expression. Gruff and enigmatic as her husband could be...he was rather sweet in his own way.

His thumb stroked over her jaw. "I want this to be over, so we can be alone."

"Because...pounding?" Her smile died, trying to assign any sort of good connotation to that word.

His own lip twitched, haunted by the ghost of a smile. "Those women scared you a little, didn't they?"

"Perhaps." She swallowed, turning her jaw into the cup of his palm. "But also, their voices were so..." The words hovered out of reach, nothing truly touching it until she found one that worked. "Hungry. They said they wanted you to treat them like an animal...and if that is what you want to do, then I want it too."

Though his eyes flared at her words, he didn't exactly seem pleased with the comparison.

"Honey…a wedding night is no time for a pounding," he crooned with a depth that vibrated deep, deep into her bones, landing with a slick warmth in the very center of her. "And a man should leash his animal for a virgin. Tonight, we take it slow and soft. We have the rest of our lives for anything else."

As the rough pad of his thumb traced a gentle caress up her jaw, Rosaline decided that suddenly, the rest of her life didn't seem so terrible after all.

CHAPTER 7

An animal.

Eli stood at the bedroom door not allowing himself to reach for the latch.

Goddamn right, an animal. His lust was a fucking beast with teeth and claws intent on tearing into his flesh and ripping him open.

The tragedy of it all, was that he was everything those women said about him in the bedroom. Just a creature, generally in search of a good pounding. A hard and dirty fuck, one without shame or scruples. Though pride wouldn't allow him to leave a woman unsatisfied, he'd sometimes leave them marked a little, too.

His hands were rough and strong, often pressing fingerprints into feminine flesh while they fucked. He loved to put his mouth on a woman, and sometimes his teeth, too.

If she returned the favor, even better.

God. He couldn't think like that right now. Not about his tiny, doe-eyed wife.

Instead of teeth and claws, she used guileless resourcefulness to get what she wanted today, and it had impressed the hell out of him.

Right before she broke his fucking heart.

What a selfish bastard he'd been, to kiss a lady like that and then avoid her like a coward. Like a dangerous, insatiable coward who could think about nothing but the flavor of innocence he'd tasted in her kiss. Of the lithe body she'd pressed against his.

Kissing her was the first time since he planted boots on this fucking island that he'd been warm. Her touch had set his blood on fire, and damned if he couldn't wait for it to happen again.

What stopped him from wrenching the latch and kicking the door open was the quiet desperation of her pleas on the balcony. Her fear of his ire. Her frantic need to do what it took to please him and her assumption that she'd repulsed him in the first place.

The bruises behind her eyes had been put there. Her skin was peach and perfect in every regard, but she'd been wounded by someone. She carried the kind of scars no one could see.

If he ever found out who it was, he'd put a bullet between *their* fucking eyes. But not before making them beg for the release death would provide.

The door swung open, and Eli found himself face-to-face with a strange woman burdened with a veritable metric ton of cream fabrics of every conceivable texture. He recognized the hem of the wedding dress as he stooped to gather a silk stocking she'd dropped in her surprise.

"Och, ye're an eager husband," she said in a lyrical Scottish accent before giggling and shouldering past him out the door.

Eager. The word wasn't strong enough.

His wife sat at a dressing table smoothing a brush down hair that already crackled from being tended to. It'd been a riot of intricate coils and curls earlier but had relaxed into sleek waves that fell down to her waist.

Eli stood in the doorway reminding himself to

breathe. He had to do this often around her. Like when she'd floated down the church aisle looking some kind of fairy princess, complete with a goddamn crown and everything. Women like her weren't real...and they certainly weren't *his*. She belonged in a story born of fantastical mythology, rather than this harsh and filthy world full of guile and greed.

He'd been so painfully aware that she should have been walking toward a charming prince, not a miserly Midas.

Swathed in acres of froth and cream, she'd been so ethereally beautiful, it had physically hurt to look at her. She shone like the desert sun, her light reflecting off everyone and everything it touched.

And she didn't even know it. She didn't see the masculine eyes that followed her every step. Didn't hear the envy other men portrayed when congratulating him. Didn't mark the jealousy of women who might outrank her but were far beneath her in every respect.

Beautiful blueberry eyes met his in the mirror of the dressing table, and they stayed like that for a time. Every hair on his body lifted as a strange voltage forked through the space between them. Women had greeted him naked before, and hadn't had the effect she did in her modest, high-necked nightgown that shimmered in the lanternlight and did enchanting things to the luster of her hair.

Eli had chosen this room in Hespera House because he'd enjoyed the dark, masculine blues and coppers, the air eternally seasoned with scents of Moroccan leather, wood polish, and freshly laundered linens.

Looking around it now, he was surprised not to find it drenched in honeysuckle vines, so pleasant was the feminine florals that seemed to drift with her everywhere. She was so out of place here, so pale and unabashedly female among all the dark wood and heavy leather.

She rotated her shoulders to welcome him with a genuine smile that made him a bit light-headed. "Do come in, Mr. Wolfe."

His body obeyed her edict before he'd made the decision to, all but stumbling forward until he stood in the middle of the room like a supplicant summoned before a goddess.

"I feel like you should call me Eli, as we're married and all."

Her smile flexed with amused chagrin. "And you should call me Rosaline, then. Or Ros if you'd rather, as my family often does."

"Rosaline..." The name felt nice on his tongue.

She giggled. "I like how you say it in your accent. Long instead of crisp."

"That right?" He felt a smile tugging at the corner of his own tight expression, as she charmed him into a more comfortable stance. He liked her accent too.

And she'd say his name often, if he had anything to do with it.

"It's been a long day," she sighed. "You look tired."

And she looked fresh as a fucking spring daffodil.

"You'll have to get used to that, a husband old as me," he teased, rubbing at eyes that felt gritty as sandpaper and twice as heavy. "These lines never disappear no matter how much sleep I get."

"I don't mind, you know," she said.

"Mind what?"

"Your lines. I noticed the crow's feet branching from your eyes, and the brackets around your mouth that deepen when you're angry or amused. I think they're dignified." She set her brush on the dressing tabletop. "I find I enjoy the character they lend your features more than the smooth faces of boys. You're more striking to look at."

Striking to look at. He'd been called worse things. Almost sounded like a compliment. He was at least glad he didn't disgust her.

"And you look..." Every word that crowded in his mouth refused to be released. He'd not the most impressive vocabulary in the world, but damned if every word for pretty he ever learned didn't occur to him all at once. "You look too fancy for sleeping."

Shit, had he really just said that out loud?

Eli'd been a wealthy man for eight years, and filthy rich for just longer than four. He was more or less used to luxury now. He sometimes spent his money on accommodating women or expensive accommodations. On food and travel, et cetera. But his wife...she was something else.

Refinement, sophistication, *and* intellect. That old bastard Crompton had been right; money couldn't purchase what she possessed, the innate elegance that dripped from every smooth, soft, graceful inch of her.

She was an extravagance for a man like him. An unobtainable dream.

And he was nothing but a stone-skinned ogre who'd never learned what to do in the moments he wasn't working.

Looking down, he catalogued the calluses on every crease of his thick fingers, on the pads of his palms. The scars on his knuckles.

Was he really going to put these hands on her?

Rosaline stood and turned to face him, allowing her wrapper to slide from her shoulders.

His heartbeat stumbled, causing the subsequent ones to collide into each other, abandoning all semblance of rhythm.

The high neck of the nightgown was diabolically deceptive, as the filmy fabric flowed down over her body in a gossamer whisp of nothing.

He'd planned to undress her slowly tonight, to get used to one part before discovering the next.

But *that* fucking thing revealed it all. The pucker of

her pert, peach nipples in the November chill, the long line of her tiny waist, the little dark shadow between her legs.

Every scruple he ever had immediately disintegrated in the inferno that scored through his blood and landed in his loins. Retreating to the bed to put it between them, he steadied himself on the post until the wave of vertigo abated. There was no denying it now. Goddammit, neither of them would sleep tonight until his hands had corrupted every innocent inch of her.

"Where the fuck did you get that gown?" he croaked.

"The seamstress asked if I wanted anything alluring for the wedding night, and when she found this, I couldn't seem to help myself." She plucked at where it draped against her hip, fluffing it like a new ballgown. "Do you like it?"

"Honey. I like it so much I need to stay over here a while."

She tilted her head. "Why?"

Because that godforsaken garment was little thicker than a moonbeam, and illuminated everything that drove him out of his goddamned mind. "I'm reminding certain parts of myself that they need to behave."

"Which parts?" She took a step toward him.

"Oh, you'll know which parts here in a bit."

"You are not *required* to behave with your wife," she reminded him, an unholy mischief glimmering in her eyes.

His hand tightened so hard on the wooden bedpost, he feared it might snap off in his grip. "Don't go saying shit like that to me, woman," he warned. "Not right now."

Regarding him quizzically, she gave him a thorough examination. "You've come to bed without visiting your valet first. You're still fully dressed?"

"Good thing, too, or I'd have frightened that maid of yours."

Tilting her head back, she gave a little giggle that jostled her breasts in a way that emptied his mouth of all moisture. "Hildie doesn't frighten easily, but I'll admit I appreciate that she hasn't seen more of you."

His eyes snapped back up to her face, searching it. "That almost sounds possessive."

She shifted, threading her fingers through her hair in a nervous gesture. "I…almost feel possessive. I didn't like those women talking about what they wanted you to do to them. I am very much hopeful that you were in earnest when you claimed not to want a mistress."

Who could imagine a mistress when he'd a ripe, willing, perfect young wife right in front of him?

"I'm all yours, honey." Something in him cringed away from how true the words rang for a woman he barely knew. "Though I'd be careful what you wish for."

"All mine." She drifted closer, the steps bringing her bare thighs against the translucent fabric, the forward momentum plastering it to her alluring frame. "To have and to hold."

Why did the words sound strange now? Why did they open up some hollow ache in the cavern of his chest?

Plenty of women had had him, but none of them ever held him.

"To do with what you like." It took every ounce of self-containment to stand still and allow her to approach him. Like someone would a skittish pet.

"What I'd like…" She paused to ponder. "Since you've bypassed your valet, may I undress you?"

Suddenly he felt like he'd swallowed the salt flats east of the Nevada desert. "I'm a man full grown who has been dressing and undressing myself since I was knee high to a grasshopper. I don't want you to have to—"

"What if I want to?" she hurried. "I've never seen a man without his clothes on before. Never touched one."

A grim sympathy twisted his mouth into a wince.

"Lord am I sorry my hairy ass is going to be your first," he grumbled. "I was thinking about maybe keeping some of my clothes on so I wouldn't frighten you too much."

Her winged brows drew low over a bemused expression. "You think you're frightening naked?"

"I mean… I've intimidated a few people here and there." He shrugged, squeezing at a gathering tension behind his neck.

"Because you're big."

He choked, fairly certain she wasn't speaking about his pecker.

"There's that, sure, but I more thought someone innocent as you might be a bit… I don't know, overwhelmed by the whole—by all of me."

Her face broke into a brilliant smile, and the earth stood still to see it. "It's the fact that you consider such things that keeps me from being thusly overwhelmed."

Thusly. He would never stop liking the way she talked. And good God, was she taking long enough to cross the room, it might as well have been the Thames. It was all he could do not to storm over there, toss her over his shoulders, and chuck her on the bed.

"You said I was your first kiss," he mentioned, shoving that impulse away.

"I did."

"And your first naked man."

"You are."

"What about come, Rosaline? Have you ever done that?"

She paused and he almost punched himself in the face for asking something that broke her concentration. "Come where?"

Oh shit. "I'm asking if you've ever…touched yourself." His eyes flicked to the shadowy triangle at the apex of her creamy thighs. "There."

That head tilt again. "I don't see how one could go through life without at least a cursory—"

"That isn't what I mean," he said, grabbing his growing impatience with both hands. "Have you ever explored that place, felt what your fingers could do? Have you ever experienced the kind of pleasure that keeps you prisoner in your own body?"

Her bafflement visibly deepened. "I'm sure I would have remembered something like that."

"Not even when washing?" God the idea of her in the bath, eyes closed. Lips parted. Fingers toying with her sweet sex.

A little guilty color tinged her cheeks and threatened to drive him out of his fucking mind. "Sometimes... there's an... Oh, I don't know what to call it. An ache? Something vibrating and insistent. Something I was told was wicked."

"Oh, it's wicked, all right." And tonight, it would be downright sinful.

Her eyes went wide, luminous even, as she closed the gap between them. "Prudence told me if were to...to share a bed, I needed to expect a paroxysm of pleasure, but she said it was your responsibility to...to do it to me."

"Goddamned right, it is."

Nodding as if that was settled, she lifted her hands to his shirt. "May I?"

"So polite," he murmured. "I almost regret you'll get over it someday."

"I'll always be polite."

"Not to me, you won't. Just wait." One day, she'd be feisty and frank and filthy as she held the reins to their fucking. That would be a thing to behold.

Her skeptical smile charmed the shit out of him as deft fingers fell to his buttons and popped them free with infuriating deliberation. The rasp of the fine cotton over his skin, the motions of her fingers, so close to his flesh above the barrier of the garment. It made every one of his hairs individuate with appreciation.

"You're killing me on purpose, aren't you, honey?" he accused on a groan.

Shaking her head, she freed the last one. "I rather like that you call me honey. I've never heard that endearment before, and it makes me feel as though you think I'm sweet."

"You're just about the sweetest thing alive... And I know you've honey yet to be discovered." He could almost taste it. Sweet and salty and slick on his tongue.

It was an infuriating and oddly erotic thing not to touch her. She needed his gentility. His patience. And if he got his hands on her, he might snag that pretty fabric or rend the garment in two. So he waited. Watched.

Wanted.

Rather than parting his open shirt, her hands slid inside the opening to test the texture of his chest.

They both gasped when her fingertips landed, and she snatched them away with an uncertain little peek up at him through her lashes. "This...is still all right?"

"Do what you want," he gritted through his teeth.

She regarded him skeptically, the fingers on the bedpost gone white with strain, the muscles in his jaw tight enough to chisel iron from rock, the sheen of concentration and restraint blooming on his brow.

"Are you certain? You look as if you are in agony."

He bared his teeth in what he hoped was a smile. "It's the best kind of agony there is."

"I'll never understand Americans," she muttered good-naturedly as she returned to her discovery of him.

Shaped and manicured nails slid through a whorl of crisp dark hair on his chest, making the whole of himself bristle and shiver as desire rioted through every nerve, vein, and sinew of his being. When she finally flattened her palms over his pectorals, he did his best to control the twitches and jumps his muscles made at the sensation of her touch.

She didn't stay still for long; her hands roamed across the planes of his chest, gliding over the flats of his nipples in a way that made him bite his cheek so hard he tasted blood. She charted a course upwards, finally parting the shirt and easing it over the swells of his shoulders and down.

The tightly knit cords and grooves of his arms seemed to transfix her as she explored some of the roping veins along the length of them.

Before his shirt became a puddle on the floor, she'd lifted the backs of her knuckles to trail down the obdurate ripples of his ribs before discovering his abdominals. "I didn't know one could count these," she said just above a whisper, dragging a fingertip over each corrugation. "Three on each side."

His teeth were set so deep he was afraid he might crack one, so he finally allowed his jaw to relax enough to reply. "I guess I'm on the lean side of large."

"I'm lean." She stepped back to look down at herself. "But I haven't such definition." A hand floated over her belly, where it curved beneath the navel with a quivering softness.

Fuck. *Fuck* he was going to lose his control before she even undid his pants.

Maybe he *should*... Maybe it was best he relieve himself once so he didn't shove a cock *this* hard and hot into her virginal flesh.

"Goodness," she said with a whisper he'd only heard in a church. "You're so..."

When she trailed off, he found a few helpful descriptors. "Cumbersome? Rough? Unwieldy?"

"Exquisite," she finished. "I'd commission a statue, but I'm convinced you're already crafted from warm stone."

Never in his life had Eli blushed, but goddamned if he didn't feel red from his toes tothe tips of his ears.

When her hands fell to the band of his trousers, he covered them with his own, pulling her away. "I lied. I can't take this," he confessed. He was hollowed out with longing. A bit more of his decency and humanity carved away with each innocent caress. "These come off and I'm...well, I'm liable to forget myself."

She took a moment to search his eyes, and he could see the exact moment she glimpsed that beast of teeth and claws snarling for a taste of her. Baying to rip her legs open and shove inside of her, claiming her as his own.

Nodding, she let him go and backed away slowly, instinctively knowing not to trigger his predatory instincts.

When the backs of her legs found the bed, she flattened her palms behind her and lifted her backside to rest on the blue velvet coverlet. She sat and studied him, those big eyes alert but not wary. "If you are in need, you can just, get on and—"

"Hush," he said more sharply than intended as he kicked off his uncomfortable dress shoes and peeled away his trousers, leaving his underthings slung low on his waist.

The creamy cotton did little to hide the shape of his erection, but the barrier was needed for now.

"Look at you," he breathed.

"I can't" she answered just as breathlessly, her gaze drifting over him to snag on what was happening below his waist. "I can't stop looking at you."

A tenderness underscored the surge of unmitigated need that swamped him as he gazed down at her body, draped in that filmy, silky, shimmering bit of magic someone had the nerve to call a nightgown.

"I'm going to put my mouth on you," he warned.

"Yes." She planted her hands behind her, leaning back to lift her face toward his. "Kiss me."

He came to the bed, standing over her. Feeling like some pagan god about to consume a virginal sacrifice. Cupping her chin in his hand, he was reminded that her bones were delicate as spun glass. "No, little wife. I'm not just going to kiss you, I'm going to devour every secret inch of you. I'm going to taste you in ways you might not yet have imagined, and I want you to make peace with that right now."

Her face warmed right there in the palm of his hand, turning a brighter shade that he'd yet seen. She swallowed once, twice, the subtle movement of her graceful throat working against his hand.

Once her chin dipped in a nod of acquiescence, he was lost.

She met his kiss with a warm, sibilant welcome, and what he tasted inside of her mouth set his skin on fire.

Need. As big and vital as his, trapped in a much smaller frame.

Nothing else in the world existed outside of her tantalizing flavor. The kiss was all soft groans and silken slides, giving way to penetrating explorations and hot, seductive swirls.

Eli's lungs felt as if they'd dilated to twice their size in order to take in the frantic breaths they shared, locking them away as part of himself. Yearning to become part of her with such fanatical fervency, he could feel the throbbing of his cock in the curl of his toes, the arteries of his wrists, the chamber in his chest.

His body was one huge, synchronous heartbeat, and he kissed her as if she could save him from this excruciating craving.

Breaking the kiss, she whispered against his lips, "Stop being so careful, Eli. I'm not as fragile as everyone thinks."

The dam of his self-control shattered, and his hands were on her before she'd finished her admonition. In the past, he'd gone right for the good stuff. Breasts, ass, thighs, pussy, usually in that order.

But, as in all things, Rosaline was different than any other woman.

His fingers found the oddest places wildly erotic. A downy trail behind her ear that led along her swanlike neck. The divot above her clavicles. The eruption of goosepimples hidden beneath the filmy garment as his abrasive skin snagged on her sleeves.

Their lips continued to shape and morph against one another, their heads constantly repositioning as their tongues tested, advanced, retreated, teased.

Eli couldn't remember why he'd not been fond of kissing before.

Perhaps because no one had tasted like her before. No one had so artlessly and amorously endeared herself to him, so much that he cared enough to indulge in this time-consuming exploration of her gentle mouth, one designed for sin and sensation.

Perhaps he'd be her first lover, but she was his first, too.

The first woman who'd ever shaped both her palms to his jaw and held it as if it were precious. The first to thread elegant fingers into his hair to stroke and sift rather than pull and demand. The first to ever use a word like "exquisite" to describe him.

The first to make him burn with such intensity, the heat threatened to melt the fortress of iron he'd cast around his heart.

Eventually, his hand found her breast, tested the soft curve of it, kneaded the insignificant weight. He cupped the entire thing in his palm and still spanned some of her ribs with his fingers.

The shape of her body wasn't sloped and gathered into dramatic peaks and valleys. They reminded him of the difference between the Rocky Mountains and the pastoral hills of this country. Gentle curves, seamlessly rolling into the next with unmeasured perfection. Easily explored, endlessly lovely. Soft where a woman should be soft, but sleek in an almost feline manner.

When his thumb grazed the taut nipple, she gasped against his mouth and squeezed her thighs shut. Smiling with a sensual suspicion, he did it again, delighted when her hips twitched and squirmed where she sat.

"You feel that, don't you?" he crooned, pressing little kisses against the corners of her mouth, the bridge of her nose, the divot in her chin.

"How could I not?" she whispered back.

"You feel it between those pretty thighs," he pressed. "When I do this."

Her breath hitched as he thrummed the other nipple, using the fabric to produce the soft glide his skin could not.

"*Yes*," she rasped. "How do you do that?"

"That's all you, honey." He kissed her temples, her fluttering eyelids, the sharp peaks of her cheekbones. "So responsive."

Though he tried to keep his kisses gentle, they deepened each time his mouth returned to hers. Slow, consuming ardor intensified to strong sweeps of his tongue, a rhythmic intrusion echoing what his body yearned to do to hers.

Demanding her surrender, thrilling when she submitted.

He moved on before he went too deep, dragging his lips down her throat, over the gossamer gown, his hands also venturing lower to make way.

With a broken sigh, she lowered from her hands to her elbows, offering the flesh his mouth sought in an erotic arch of her spine.

He bent over her, his lips finding her tight nipple and

kissing it, dampening the fabric as he opened them to use it as a filter for his hot breath.

"Oh... Oh my—" Her whisper was lost to a moan as his tongue flicked over it, his hand shaping to the curve of her waist, her trembling hip. The flimsy fabric often caught on his calluses, the sound of the scrape a ripping reminder of what he did to delicate things.

She didn't seem to have a care for the garment, as her hips rolled slightly forward, lifting toward his hand's approach as if upon instinct.

Regardless of the welcome, her thighs were still clamped tight as a vise. Mouth never leaving her breast, he traced the seam where her thigh met her torso, following it to the downy patch between her legs.

He pet her idly, enjoying the feel of the intimate hair beneath the web of see-through silk.

"Eli?"

He heard every question contained in the single syllable of his name, and he lifted her head to meet her anxious, unfocused gaze. "I'm right here with you. Just lie back and let me make you feel good."

"Should I...should I be doing something?"

"I'll tell you what to do," he said.

"Oh. Good." Relaxing, she allowed her shoulder blades to meet the mattress, arms straight at her sides, gripping the coverlet as if it would keep her from falling.

Eli reclined on one elbow beside her, nuzzling at the fragrant cove between her neck and her hair, breathing in honeysuckle and the warm, intoxicating musk of her skin.

Resting his hand on the flat of her stomach, he marveled at how far across it spanned. Hipbone to hipbone, maybe a little more. This time, he paid attention to her other breast, teasing the fabric with his damp breath, kissing, licking, and laving.

His hand smoothed down the plane of her stomach again, to stroke over the slight curve of her mons.

This time, she melted on a sigh.

Eli stretched the moment as long as it would allow, playing softly against the plump furrows of flesh with lazy strokes, and tickling the tightly closed slit from over the fabric.

Encouraged by her soft little expressions of air and the visible twitches and trembling of her thighs, he slid his index finger into the crease of her sex. Fingertip covered in silk, he found the slight protrusion of her nub, and bent his finger around it, gliding toward those pliant folds of protective skin.

It was between those folds he found a pool of slick heat.

Sweet. Holy. Christ. She was so fucking wet.

This was something a diligent wife couldn't pretend. This evidence of her body's desire, this slick concoction only a woman's well could spring to make ready for his intrusion.

She stiffened, as if suddenly aware of the situation.

"Oh," she fretted. "Oh no. Something is wrong."

Lifting his head from her breast, he said, "No, my sweet wife. Everything is all right."

"But—"

"It's supposed to happen…" he soothed. "So I can do this." Coating the fabric and his finger with the moisture, he drew it up through both layers of her sex until he found the fold he sought.

She jolted as if struck by lightning. Her teeth audibly clacked together, and legs straightened into the nether past the edge of the bed, her toes curled into tight little buttons.

He rotated the insinuated finger this way and that as he returned to stroke and suck at her nipple with his mouth.

"Oh," she breathed again. "It's never felt so...ah!" Her back arched off the bed as he ever so gently scraped his teeth against the taut peak while simultaneously threading his finger just beneath the hardened little pearl.

Eli released her nipple, gaping down in disbelief as she bowed up in a supple arc, as if someone had tied marionette strings to her sternum. A high, tight sound escaped as her hips convulsed in strong, brief jerks.

Could she really be this sensitive? Was she truly coming apart after only a couple of twists and touches?

Her throat made little grunts and groans of distress until one of her hands slapped against her mouth, and her teeth bit down on the middle finger.

Wide, wet eyes found him as he continued the miniscule movements of his fingers. He stayed with her, his eyes boring down into hers. Doing his best to convey what he was incapable of saying. That the sight of her pleasure humbled him more than would the presence of God. That he was grateful she broke into his observatory because that led them to this moment. That he was beginning to feel things he couldn't identify.

Things he didn't dare profane with something so base as language.

She must have found what she sought, because she gave over to the moment, allowing little tremors to wrack through her until she brought her knees up in order to twist and writhe away from a climax gone too sensitive to bear any longer.

Eli took pity on her, pulling his hand away.

"I—I never knew," she marveled. "I never... Oh no. What—"

Taking advantage of her movement, he nudged at her bent knees, encouraging her to part them. When she resisted, he increased the pressure.

"Open for me, sweetheart," he begged. "I have to taste you."

She lay back, looking up at the canopy, her chest heaving for breaths. "Something…happened. I can feel it. Everywhere. It's too much."

"I know, darlin', but I'll be gentle."

"You can't see," she said, gripping her knees tighter. "Perhaps I should just…get a cloth or something. Oh please, don't look. It'll disgust you."

Eli bit into his knuckle before he could conjure a reply, clamping his teeth hard enough to nearly break the skin. The pain centered him a little, kept him from just expiring from a scarcity of blood to any extremity but one.

She wasn't talking about the pleasure being too much. But what the pleasure did to her.

"Rosaline." He looked down, his chest aching a little at the embarrassment etched into the crease of her brow. "You're gonna need to trust me, honey. I want you as wet and slippery as you can get, and I'll prove that to you just as soon as you open up for me."

Chewing on her cheek, she hesitated, then he felt her resistance abate, and she allowed him to spread her milk-white thighs open.

It was everything Eli could do not to pass out on the spot.

Beneath the swath of fabric, darkened in the place he'd dipped into the pool of her desire, her core bloomed like a rose in a rainstorm. Glistening with the aftermath of her come.

The first of the night.

Eli positioned himself between her legs, preventing her trembling knees from closing with the width of his shoulders.

"My gown," she whispered through a hand still pressed against her mouth.

Lifting enough to find the hem, he rolled it up her legs, kissing every exposed inch of her. Even here he found the oddest things to appreciate. The graceful arch of her foot, the nibs of her active little toes, curling and stretching with overwrought sensation. Her ankle was delicate, her calves long, her knee smooth with an eminently kissable little dimple beside it.

Lord but she was soft, especially here on the insides of her thighs where tiny blue veins threaded beneath thinner, impossibly smoother skin.

He sucked in a breath through his teeth as he lifted the veil of her nightgown above her waist.

When the instinctive clamp of her knees was thwarted by his shoulders, she reached down to cover herself.

One hand over her mouth. The other over her sex.

This instinct was wrong. Was a product of what the world did to a woman. Made her ashamed of her sounds and her sex. Both of which, he craved.

Doing his best to put her at ease, he kissed and nuzzled, nudged and cajoled. Her knuckles, the valley between her fingers where the damp cove beckoned. "Do not hide from me, honey," he said darkly. "Do not deny me a taste of heaven."

"You can't possibly want—"

His head snapped up as he rippled with dominant need. "I'll tell you what I want."

She visibly swallowed.

"I want you to put your hands down at your sides," he ordered on a barely contained growl. "I want to hear you come apart beneath my mouth. I want you to sing my name. To scream it to those stars you like so much. To sob and cry and beg with abandon. Without shame. I want you to writhe and buck beneath my face. To ride my lips like you would a wild pony. I want a river of your come in my mouth, and when I finally fuck you, I want it to drench my cock, as well."

"Stop," she breathed, both hands lifting to cover her

face, exposing her sex to him once again. "You're too wicked. I'll do what you want, but say no more."

"Then. Put. Your. Hands. Down."

She obeyed him, threading her trembling fingers into the velvet coverlet.

Taking pity on her, he smoothed his lips over her inner thighs, breathing in her distinct, feminine fragrance. Swallowing the rush of moisture his mouth produced.

He took a moment to just look at her, to appreciate the delicate, glistening ruffles of her sex. She was compact and contained in a little cove of wispy dark curls as sweet and small as the rest of her. Pleasure and a very masculine sort of pride lanced through him, filling even the spaces between his heartbeats, carrying one truth with it.

Mine.

Entranced, Eli parted her with reverent fingers, exposing her thoroughly. The pink, swollen flesh at her core pulsed and clenched at emptiness.

He would fill her soon enough.

But first, he'd make her scream his name.

He nuzzled his mouth into soft flesh no other man had been blessed enough to enjoy, with a bone-deep purr of satisfaction. Licking her open with the flat of his tongue, he tasted her recent pleasure, a skein of moist, feminine silk.

She gasped and trembled, her hands again fisting in the coverlet, draining of all color.

But her thighs fell truly apart in hopeless capitulation.

Eli's tongue slithered and slid through pliant ridges of quivering flesh, devouring her flavor, warm dark honey and liquid desire. He soaked his lips with it, trailing from the secreted bud all the way down to the entrance of her body from which the spring still flowed.

He fluttered there for a moment, testing the tight ring

with the tip of his tongue, prodding it enough to feel the muscles clench with the rhythm of her own racing heart.

Fuck she was tight. He pressed again at her core, laving and loving it, until a hand clenched in his hair, and she made a plaintive little moan.

He smiled against her sex, knowing more than she did, it seemed, what she was asking him to do.

Flattening his tongue, he split the seam of her inner folds and brushed the bundle of nerves they protected with a featherlight flick.

His wife's hips left the bed, and she tossed her head to release a sob to the sky.

Pinning her thighs open with a splay of his hands, he grazed the bud again, and a third time, reveling in the little mewls she made, in the writhing of her limbs as she both sought to encourage and escape what was coming for her.

I could love you.

Eli disengaged with a wet, wicked sound. His breath coming in tight rasps.

Her adorable ass fell back to the bed, her thighs still splayed indecently beneath his hands.

He didn't own the thought. Sure, it was in his own head. In his own voice. But it wasn't his. Never would he think something so batshit crazy while supping between a woman's legs.

He stared down at her, her long hair fanned out like a cloud of silk over velvet. Her lips puffy and glossy from his kisses. Her nipples dark beneath the damp circles he'd made of her gown, contrasting with the prim pallor of the rest of her.

She watched him through eyes half-lidded, meeting his own startled gaze.

I could love you.

What had even conjured such nonsense? And why had it intruded into this? Here? Now?

That little voice didn't know what the fuck it was talking about.

He didn't know shit from shit when it came to love. Didn't really believe in it. People succumbed to desire and called it love. They wanted to own someone just like he owned things, and the only legal way to do that these days was to lock them into marriage contracts.

Like this one.

Lithe little fingers slid over the ones he'd splayed on her thighs, threading into the negative spaces, curling into the dips between his knuckles and nudging them wider so they could insinuate between each and interlock together.

With that small, earnest gesture. That one quiet, lovely action, she'd managed to stop the entire world from turning. To quiet his qualms and melt something that'd been solid and cold for as many years as he could remember.

What replaced it wasn't exactly as tender as expected.

It was that damned beast. The one cursed with eternal hunger. It filled him with instincts as possessive and primal as he could imagine. Violent ardor. Uncontrolled adoration.

He needed to fuck her deep. To shape that tight channel of wet flesh to his body and his, alone. To put a baby inside of her. Hell, a whole fucking blueberry-eyed brood if she wanted, tumbling around like that litter of kittens, squalling and screeching through the palace he was going to build her.

Because he was a creature obsessively loyal to ritual. He found a food he liked the most and consumed it almost exclusively. He wore the fabrics he liked against his skin, regardless of cost. He'd kept the same friends for thirty years. Drank the same scotch, smoked only one brand of cigar. Not for any particular reason, he was just squirted into this world that way.

Sure, he'd no concept of love, but once he developed a taste...he returned to taste it again and again.

Licking his lips, he savored the elixir she'd left there before hunkering down for more.

His poor little wife...

She really had no idea what she was in for.

CHAPTER 8

Rosaline was lost in an enchantment of sensation wreathed in delectable darkness. At first, she'd squirmed from it, awash with shame. She'd truly known nothing of this act but the bare bones of what went where.

And every moment had been one pleasant shock after another.

Not the least of which was the large, virile creature that was her husband.

He stood at the foot of the bed, towering over her prone, exposed body. Her thighs clamped open by his formidable hands.

He looked perfectly savage.

Butterflies danced low in her belly as he gazed down at her like some arrogant god, rapacious as a winter wolf resplendent with lupine grace.

If only her very first climax hadn't stolen her ability to form coherent sentences. She might have told him how magnificent he looked just now. His surplus of muscle locked with tension, the gold of the lantern gilding the fine, crisp fleece on his chest and illuminating the arrow it made down his large torso before disappearing into his waistband. With all his talk of being rough, she found most of his skin surprisingly smooth. She'd tell him that someday. Someday when he wasn't looking down at her as if trying to decide which part of her to devour first.

Instead, she laced their fingers together on her parted thighs, drawing them wider, higher, offering herself as an altar to his abiding lust. Wishing he'd not ceased the magic he wrought with his mouth.

Who knew her body had been capable of such consuming pleasure?

As if reading her mind, he settled back between her legs, spreading the folds of her sex once more with that seeking, probing, *oh so* skillful tongue of his.

He was slow. Relentless. Teasing and tasting as if he'd no sense of how the little bud of her sex was desperate for this inexorable tension to spill over into release.

His breath was hot, feathery and his movements sinuous and ultimately sensual as she did her best not to squirm and writhe this way and that in order to get him just where she needed. To that place he always seemed unable to find.

Yes. Right there. No. *There.* No, dammit, if he'd hold his head bloody still, she'd just find it for him and—what had he called it?

Ride my lips like a wild pony.

She couldn't imagine that she would at the time, but that was before he insisted on making her work this hard to keep him where he ought to stay.

Thus far he'd been a dominant lover, and she'd found that soothed her fears. Now he seemed intent on driving her mad. He'd slide through slippery, pliant flesh making strange, possessive noises. Whispering words against her sex she couldn't imagine, let alone identify. But when it seemed he would approach the place that promised to turn this throbbing torment into another soul-searing, earth-shattering climax, he danced away.

If she didn't know better, she would think he tortured her on purpose.

Upon one such disappointing maneuver, she'd released his hand to clutch at his hair and guide him the minute distance to the left that she needed.

A low, growling chuckle vibrated against her, hiking her demanding need even higher.

"I'm being cruel, aren't I?" he asked between scintillating licks. "Having my fun with you, forgetting how fevered you are. How fucking easy it is to send you over the edge."

"It's not easy," she panted, the muscles in her belly burning and trembling with strain. Her thighs quivering from the endless tightening and releasing. "I've been trying so hard."

"I know." He sucked at the little flanges of flesh with a wicked, distressingly wet sound. "Your pussy is just so pretty. So fucking delicate and delicious." He dipped his tongue low, so low against the place that throbbed and clenched around emptiness.

"Please," she whispered, hating the plaintive note in the word, though it seemed to ignite an ungodly light in his dark eyes.

"This is why you are dangerous," he groaned as he traced a sinuous trail up the inside of her thigh. "Because, it seems, I can't deny you a goddamned thing."

His mouth returned to the exact crest of flesh he'd been avoiding. Kissing and suckling, balancing her on the edge of a frighteningly tall precipice.

A gentle pressure distracted her from flinging herself over the cliff with wild, willful abandon.

A fingertip. Testing her tensile opening. Probing forward, sliding *inside*.

Her every muscle tightened at the intrusion, at the foreign nature of the sensation. Dear lord, if his finger felt this big, how was she going to take the girth of what pressed against the fabric of his underthings?

All thoughts of worry evaporated as his tongue found a magical spot, sucking her entire hood into the heat of his mouth. She gave a hoarse cry as her hips left the bed, working his finger deeper. Deeper. Until his knuckle rested against her.

He stroked her from the inside, finding places that made her gasp and writhe, lifting her again toward the precipice.

Right as she spied the edge in the distance, his clever finger pulled out of her, eliciting a sob of frustrated desperation.

Almost immediately the pressure returned, gliding wetly inside. Only this time the intrusion was more insistent, stretching her with patient but relentless pressure.

He'd added another finger.

"Christ, you're tight," he rasped.

She opened her mouth to apologize, but then his lips did something so incredible she could only sob his name in absolute wonder. Moaning, she tilted and strained against him, twisted her hips and dug her heels into the bed.

He stayed right there with her, gliding those thick fingers against her most intimate flesh, his tongue flicking and sucking at the place where all nerves seemed to coalesce.

Stars exploded behind her eyes, blinding her with brilliant, white-hot pleasure that flirted with electric pain. She was catapulted into the cosmos, flung past beloved constellations whose appellations she'd somehow lost. There was only one name she could remember, and it was torn from her tongue in helpless pants and ebullient sobs.

And, finally, in quiet, quivering cries for mercy.

A mercy he granted by abandoning her altogether.

She collapsed to the bed, a boneless puddle of pleasure, still plagued by the occasional thrill and pulse that animated her limbs.

How it was possible to be both empty and replete, she wasn't certain, but the entrance to her body still felt dilated and demanding.

He left her for only a moment, returning to bend over her and draw the soaking nightgown over her head. She was as limp as that empty gown, limbs heavy with a lovely exhaustion.

"Yes," he murmured, his big body hovering above her. "Just float there, honey. Stay relaxed if you can."

He lowered himself with infinite care, freezing at some point as if capable of doing nothing more than working breath in and out of his lungs.

She managed the strength to lift her hand to his shoulder "What is it?"

"I've never felt so fucking heavy in my life," he muttered. "I'm going to crush you." His arms flexing with a shift in weight, he made to leave. "I should stand," he gritted out. "Safer."

"No." Suddenly she was attached to him, both arms and legs, wrapped around him like a barnacle. "I…I think I need you here," she said in a small voice. "Close."

Pressing a gentle kiss to her temple, he settled against her incrementally.

He *was* heavy. His torso pressing her thighs impossibly wide. His chest abrading hers with crisp hair. The hard planes of his body forcing her soft ones to yield.

It was glorious.

Something the approximate texture and temperature of a branding iron rested against her thigh.

Oh my. He'd left her to relieve himself of the last barrier between them and, apparently, wipe her essence from his lips before returning to kiss her.

He tasted different this time. Heady with a salty musk

she recognized as her own. It wasn't entirely unpleasant, this reminder of what he'd just done to her.

For her.

Surely she'd been the only one to succumb to such searing pleasure. And, though he seemed to enjoy himself, he'd not had his own climax yet.

That, she could not abide.

She wanted this. Wanted him to find ease in her body. Wanted to grant him at least a modicum of the pleasure he'd given her.

When he didn't take it, she broke the kiss to gaze up at him, her husband. Her man of no mean experience. His features etched with an agony she didn't think he enjoyed any longer.

"I can't seem to bring myself to hurt you."

Heart expanding until she felt it might burst out of her chest, she wriggled her body lower, bringing her sex and his in closer proximity.

"It is best, I think, to simply plunge in like one would a cold body of water," she postulated. "Better than extending any unpleasantness with hesitation."

He closed his eyes, nodding as if she'd given sage advice, then reached down between their bodies.

What he pressed against the vulnerable opening of her body was big, blunt, and astonishingly smooth. Almost like glass heated in the sun. It slid forward ever so slightly and the pressure was instantly enormous.

Winding her arms around his neck, she pulled him in tight. Not for a kiss, but keen for a spot in which to bury her face. Finding it in the smooth arc where his shoulder met his neck.

"Do please hurry," she whispered. "If it's not too much trouble."

He coughed out something like a laugh. "So. Polite."

Then he surged forward, scalding her with a stretching, inescapable pain.

She hadn't realized her teeth had sunk into the meat of his muscle until his raw noise tore through the air, containing every bit as much pain as she felt.

Unclenching her jaw, she released his trapezius, placing a conciliatory kiss on the indentations she'd left. "I'm sorry," she whispered against his ear, soothing a hand down his rippling back.

"Don't fucking dare apologize," he croaked. Holding himself as perfectly still as his quivering muscles seemed to allow. "Jesus fucking Christ, woman."

It felt extra blasphemous for him to curse just so while seated so deeply inside of her, but she secretly liked it. It felt like a wickedness, what they'd done today. One or two extra sins wouldn't make much of a difference in the grand scheme of things.

Already the pain was beginning to abate, and Rosaline brought her awareness to where they were joined. A throbbing had intensified there, but she wasn't certain if it was her flesh or his that pulsed so persistently.

Silent seconds ticked by, and the pressure inside of her morphed from a sting to an ache to nothing more than a sharp sort of stretch. Still he did nothing. Just held himself there, his trembling intensifying as he kept his face buried in her hair. "Tell me—tell me you're all right." The words seemed to have to work their way past the strained cords she could feel in his neck.

"I'm very well." She smoothed her palms down his back once more, enjoying the way he purred like a giant cat. "It's only that...well, is one of us supposed to be moving?"

"Can't," he groaned.

"Why not?"

"Too tight."

"Oh." She did her best to make herself less tight, stretching her intimate muscles. Relaxing them as best she could, which only seemed to make things worse for him. Patting his back gently, she turned her head to place a kiss to his stubbled jaw. "I'm sorry."

"Apologize again and see what I—" His threat dissipated as her intimate muscles seemed to convulsively need to clamp and release the hardness inside of her. Dismayed, she watched his skin flush a shade she'd not yet seen.

"I can't help it," she said. "I'm—" She pressed her lips together, biting back the word. "I didn't know it would hurt you, too."

"Hurt *me*?" Another bitter sound of mirth escaped him. "Being still inside of you…it's better than the most frenzied fuck. Better than the first time."

That lit a gentle flame of pride inside of her. She didn't like the thought of him—er—fucking anyone with frenzy or otherwise. But it was quite a miraculous balm to know she surpassed those experiences without even trying.

"Do you imagine it'll be better or worse if you move?" she wondered.

"I imagine it'll be over if I move," was his grim reply.

Not wanting this connection to end, she tightened her hold as if her feeble strength could stop him from leaving her if he ever took it in his mind to do so. "Not yet," she whispered, lifting her legs to lock around his, consequently pulling him deeper.

He found the strength to lift his head enough to stare down at her, concern etched into the grooves branching from his eyes. Smoothing her hair from her face, he slid an arm behind her neck, cradling her as he pressed a tender kiss to her forehead. "Don't let go," he said, more an appeal than a command. "I think you're holding all the broken pieces of me together."

That she could do.

Her sex continued to pulse and throb, contracting around him without her permission to do so.

Though he didn't move, Eli worshiped her with his mouth. Leaving no part of her face unkissed before moving to her throat. He only stopped to indulge in a quiet groan or a spine-wrenching tremble. She found that if she tilted her hips this way, or depressed them into the bed, his reactions became stronger.

"Rosaline," he groaned. "If you don't stop I—I'll—" His words died on a strangled sound as his entire frame seized with a rippling shudder. Then another. Rough tremors cording every muscle and etching his every feature in stark relief. Warmth flooded her womb, and as he jerked and shivered, she could tell he'd released his seed inside of her.

In time, it seemed to diminish its hold over him, and he carefully curled out of her before collapsing on his side with a bone-weary groan.

They stared at each other for a moment, each clearly loath to address the enormity of what had just happened between them.

Two veritable strangers. How was it possible they had shared something so incredibly profound?

Her body broke the moment for her, releasing what he'd left inside her in a warm rush. Gasping, she sat up, clenching her drenched thighs ineffectually.

"Oh right. Shit." He leapt from the bed and padded to the ewer and bowl in the corner, wetting two cloths. He covered his sex with one of them before he turned back. "Lie back, honey, and I'll wash you."

Shaking her head, Rosaline couldn't figure why she suddenly felt so shy. More vulnerable and exposed than she ever had whilst he gazed down at the most protected parts of her. "I'd prefer to do it myself."

He returned, handing her the cloth before padding to the other side of the bed where a trunk was tucked against a tall window.

Rosaline peeked at the long form of him, glimpsing

the shades of a broad back that tapered into a behind that might have been sculpted by the same artist as did Achilles in Hyde Park.

By the time she'd finished her ablutions, she retrieved her nightgown from where it had been tossed aside in a sodden heap and then abandoned it to the dressing table in lieu of her wrapper.

Turning, she found that he'd pulled a loose pair of cotton trousers over his lean hips and was a little disappointed she'd had an entire wedding night and never truly saw him naked.

For the first time since they'd met, he looked unsure. Discomfited. As if he'd no idea what to do next.

Rosaline had thought she'd feel more womanly after he'd "made a woman of her." But for some reason, she felt as young as he'd initially accused her of being. In an attempt not to advertise how needy and pathetic she'd become, Rosaline belted her wrapper and gathered her things as he pulled the corner of the bedclothes down.

This had been good. It'd been wonderful, even.

So why did she want to have a good cry?

Clutching her things to her chest, she turned to him with a practiced smile, realizing she'd never asked to see her room. "Where am I to sleep?"

"I'm turning this bed down for you," he informed her with a lazy half-smile.

"How lovely of you." She set her things back on the dresser and went to him, lifting on her tiptoes to kiss his scratchy jaw before pouncing into the center of the bed. "Where do you sleep?"

He paused. "You mean, which side of the bed?"

"I mean, in which room?"

"This one, obviously." He regarded her quizzically.

Her jaw dropped. "We're sharing a bedroom?"

"We're married, aren't we?"

She wasn't certain if she should tell him that was no sort of helpful answer.

"We are married, yes, but surely you know it's common practice for spouses to have their own rooms. I've been told it's standard with the Americans of our class, as well."

He snorted derisively and lifted a hand to smooth down his hair that she'd clutched so wildly. The motion did impressive things to his biceps. "Well, I've never studied the bedroom habits of anyone in the upper classes of either country, but where I'm from, a husband and wife share a bed. Besides, woman, it's damned cold and damp in this country, so consider it your duty to scootch over here and keep me warm."

Secretly pleased, she did exactly that, settling her shoulder blades against his chest as he gathered her close and tucked the sumptuous covers around them.

It'd begun to rain sometime in the night, and Rosaline watched the wall across from the window cry little shadow tears.

"I think I like wifely duties," she said, her sigh morphing into a jaw-cracking yawn. The cocoon of his big body provided a feeling she'd never before experienced.

Safe. Protected.

Emmett had been right. This man, rough around almost every conceivable edge, was the perfect bulwark between her and the rest of the world.

His hand traced a path down her arm. "I like you wrapped in silk," he murmured. "But I like you better in nothing at all."

"I'm too comfortable to take it off," she murmured, fighting to keep her eyes open.

He nuzzled against her hair, pressing a kiss on her crown. "Sleep then, little wife," he crooned into the dark. "Tomorrow night I'm not going so easy on you."

CHAPTER 9

Over the next three weeks, Eli learned more lessons about ladies than he had in his entire life. His woman, specifically, though she and her sisters seemed to share certain proclivities. He'd taken to carrying a notebook in his jacket pocket to jot things down as he forged his way across the mire of marriage.

Lesson #1: Ladies' wardrobes were distressingly complicated. Additionally, their shoes were among the most important parts of said wardrobe. The fact that the shoes are rarely seen beneath their elegant skirts was, apparently, neither here nor there.

Lesson #2: The pitch and the volume of a woman's greeting to another woman was directly proportionate to how long they'd been apart and how much they'd liked and missed each other. This had been most evident when Rosaline's twin sisters, Mercy and Felicity, arrived back in town not two days prior, and he was surprised the resulting noise from each Goode girl hadn't set off all the dogs in Mayfair.

Lesson #3: Tears were not always a bad thing, and silence not always good. In fact, silence could be very dangerous and sometimes a prelude to tears.

Lesson #3.5: Tears required some amalgamation of

apology, sympathy, diplomacy, and physical affection. In one case with a leering, disrespectful gardener, he was certain it also required retribution, but ultimately Rosaline had talked him down from a lethal edge, saving her bully's life. It was explained to him she appreciated and preferred his *willingness* to murder for the sake of hurt feelings but would much rather that he didn't follow through.

He'd underlined this for further discussion.

Lesson #4: The man who'd dubbed the women's mind inferior was a fucking imbecile. When faced with a problem, ladies picked it apart until a solution was found and enacted. When unable to come up with one on their own, they convened conferences wherein every little damned outcome was discussed and analyzed before the intensely opinionated gathering came to a conclusion.

After said conclusion, many women broke into smaller groups to discuss their feelings and opinions about the conclusion, much of which was not expressed during the conference, in order to avoid conflict. It was, however, expressed at length to *him* that his opinions at these conferences were about as welcome as a woman in a voting booth.

Eli'd never had much of a strong opinion on politics either way, but after a week of marriage, he'd become convinced that if women ran the world, a lot more would be accomplished and agreed upon.

And with a great deal more humanity.

Lesson #5: There were certain excursions to which he was not and never would be welcome. These included but were not limited to: the seamstress, the haberdashers, the milliners, and particular afternoon society calls where it was explained to him that *he* was most often the topic of conversation. Consequently, his physical presence would ruin the entire affair.

This, Eli didn't mind so much, as he only allowed his wife out of the bedroom under extreme duress.

Unless it was to fuck somewhere else in the house. So far, his wife had been such an enthusiastic initiate to the marriage bed, he was fairly sure she didn't attend these events to complain.

Granted, she could castigate him for a myriad of his flaws, this he knew. So, to be safe, he sent her out of the house with her eyes half-lidded and her knees wobbly from a recent come. He'd go about his business as usual, confident he'd pleasured her into forgetting any unkind thoughts she might be harboring.

Life with a woman confused, amused, pleasured and suited him so much more than he'd ever imagined. Often, when pouring over accounts of his most recent acquisitions, he'd catch an unfamiliar reflection in a mirror, taking a moment to recognize himself, grinning like the town idiot.

Much like he was doing now, reclined in the observatory at some ungodly hour, wishing his wife would bend further over the telescope.

If she did, the shirt of his she wore might just lift enough to give him a naughty view.

One would think he'd enjoyed enough of a scintillating eyeful as she'd climbed astride him for the first time. He'd harassed and goaded her into riding his face, and after that, she'd needed some help riding his cock, as her legs had nearly given out after the first couple of climaxes.

That view had been sublime. Rosaline above him, arched with pleasure, hair flung back, the long ends tickling his thighs as she bounced and bucked with sobs and cries that echoed in his mind as clearly as they'd done from the glass ceiling.

The stars weren't out tonight, but the sky reflected layers of light from the city with strange, swirling clouds that made her appear as if their passion had summoned some otherworldly storm.

Eli still wasn't convinced she was of this world.

Unable to stifle a yawn, he indulged in a full-body stretch over the cushions they'd scattered over the floor in order to enjoy an indoor winter picnic. They'd consumed all the custard and dried fruit, and put a dent in the block of hard cheese and fresh loaf of bread the maid had arranged for him in a basket, along with a lovely bottle of red.

Eli hadn't minded so much that their honeymoon was delayed, as he'd not wanted to waste time traveling that could be spent fornicating. And yet, he'd noted a shadow cross her features when her brother and his intended discussed their honeymoon at dinner the other night.

For the first week of their marriage, the Goode family had left them largely alone, allowing the couple to cosset themselves in the cocoon of their bedroom, discovering the delight and desire they'd never shared with another soul.

Eventually, Morley had called around under the guise of discussing business, which they'd not been able to do between the barrage of questions regarding the well-being of his wife.

It occurred to Eli to be insulted, but as his wife had greeted her brother-in-law glowing with a luminous smile he'd not noted before their wedding, he'd been happy to sit in smug satisfaction as she shared her conviction of their suitability.

Tonight, he'd decided to seduce her in her favorite room in the house, which had most definitely been one of his more genius ideas. Over a sensual meal, he'd allowed her to decide the destination of their honeymoon, and she'd finally landed on Norway, of all places, so she could see the northern lights.

Figured she would choose one of the coldest places on earth…

But in the afterglow of what they'd just done, he'd have offered to pull her on a dogsled around the arctic circle if that's what she wanted.

He suggested they take a small trip through Italy on their way back, and she'd enthusiastically agreed.

"We should turn in," he said over a second more merciful yawn. "If we're going to catch the early train to Devon, we'll hate ourselves if we don't get a little sleep. I'm eager to inspect my new holdings."

"I am keen to do so, as well, but I think I see a bit of sky over there." She pointed to the west, not looking up from the telescope. "What if it comes this way and there's a break in the clouds?"

He cast the sky a dubious look but didn't have the heart to say more.

"December skies are famously fickle, you know," she continued, consulting a periodical she'd opened over the logbook. "As are the Geminids."

"Those are the twin constellations, right?"

She looked over at him with approval. "The meteors that move across the twin constellations, but yes. You remembered!"

"I'm learnin', lady." He poured on the patois he knew amused her so much, scratching idly at where her nails had bit into his bare chest. "Turns out you can teach this old dog a couple of new tricks."

"I have an appreciation for the old tricks, as well," she said with a wicked grin that stopped his heart.

"Come over here then, honey, and I'll— Hey, pssst. Castor!" he hissed at a ginger kitten as it attacked what was left of the block of cheese with predatory vigor. "Git off there, you little demon." He lifted the squirmy body from their leftovers and plunked it next to a grey tabby that'd already climbed into his lap.

The two immediately went to war, and Eli was glad he'd slid back into his pants in order to protect his pecker.

"The ginger is Astrid, the calico is Castor," Rosaline corrected with a teasing smile. "So much for your memory."

"Oh. Right." He blinked over at the tiny brood that'd become lesson #8 or was it 9?

Didn't matter, he'd learned the hard way that if he ever said "no" to animals, she was just going to do what the hell she wanted anyhow. So, it was ultimately easier to accept the fact you can't have a soft-hearted wife without a few critters for her to spend her love on.

Besides, they were kinda cute when they weren't tempting him toward murder.

He eyed the other end of the rug he occupied with narrowed eyes. Sometime during their interlude, the kittens had found their way into the observatory and knocked over their open bottle of wine on the parquet floor.

That hadn't been difficult to clean, but at some point, the priceless rare carpet was forever ruined by soaked pads of little burgundy kitten paws.

And he'd not yet identified the culprit.

"I feel like one's missing." He searched the room. "Nova and Orion are by the globe over there, and I saw Ursa creep beneath the desk. I've Astrid and Castor here."

"And Pollux," she said, sweeping up another on her way to settle on the floor beside him, setting the kitten next to the brawling siblings.

"Where's that white one?" he asked.

"Draco?" She twisted this way and that, the fabric between the buttons of his shirt parting a little to give him tantalizing glances of her pert breasts. "I haven't seen him."

He tried to remember when he had ever liked to just look at a woman so much and came up empty.

"You should have named one Andromeda," he offered, allowing Castor to gnaw on the tip of his thumb with tiny teeth.

"Oh?" She lifted her brows. "It makes sense, I suppose, that you'd have a fondness for myths about dragon-slaying heroes."

He reached for her, capturing her chin beneath his thumb and forefinger, pulling her close for a kiss. "I don't know much about that, but it was the night of the Andromeda meteor shower that I discovered I'd a fondness for *you*."

Her answering smile made him light-headed.

Pulling her close, he arranged the pillows so they were both comfortable, before draping her over his chest and pulling her leg to cover his where he employed lesson #11.

Women liked to be stroked and caressed in places other than their sexual bits. A man could get a woman to acquiesce to all sorts of depravity if he spent enough time tickling the underside of her arm, the little columns beside her spine, or the divots in her lower back and the smooth curve of her hips *without* requesting sex.

He supposed it shouldn't be a discovery that women wanted to be appreciated for more than their naughtier parts, but he was ashamed to say it was... Eli wondered how many other husbands had never cottoned to this discovery and missed out on one of the more enjoyable intimacies of marriage.

Rosaline didn't seem to mind his rough skin, arching just as shamelessly as one of the kittens in search of his touch as goosepimples lifted the fine hairs on her body.

"Tell me this dragon-slaying myth," he asked, deceptively nonchalant. Was he the hero of this story? Or the dragon protecting his hoard of treasure.

"Well, the dragon-slaying myth was just a literary device to describe this sort of narrative, but remember when I told you Andromeda was a princess of Ethiopia and widely thought one of the most beautiful women in the known world? Her mother, Queen Cassiopeia, bragged that Andromeda was even more lovely than the Nereids, who were water nymphs famous for luring lustful men to their deaths."

As she spoke, sparks of intelligence and exultance danced in her blue eyes, every bit as brilliant as those stars she was so enamored with. Stars named for heroic characters, or tragic ones.

Sometimes both.

"One of these Nereids was the wife of Poseidon, the god of the sea. Upon hearing the boast, she and her sisters demanded the entire kingdom suffer for such disrespect. Benighted by Poseidon's curse, the people demanded that the king and queen sacrifice Andromeda, who immediately acquiesced to save her people. They chained her to a rock, where she was forced to suffer before the elements, waiting for the sea monster, Cetus, to claim her."

"Am I the sea monster in this story?" he asked. "Because this took a turn I wasn't expecting."

"No," she giggled. "I was getting to that. Perseus was the son of the god Zeus and a mortal woman. He'd spent his life at sea, performing superhuman feats, not the least of which was saving Andromeda from Cetus. He fell in love with her, then, and he claimed her as his bride."

"Well, that's better, then." He settled back, his fingers toying in her hair. "I still feel a tragedy coming. How did she end up in the stars? Some shitty twist of fate, I reckon."

Shaking her head, she splayed a hand over his ribs, settling her fingers in the grooves between. "In her constellation, she's depicted in the chains she wore when sacrificed because the goddess Athena was supposedly moved by her willingness to die for her people…but *I* like to remember Andromeda more than her chains, but as she was after. The first queen of Mycenae. A woman who was loved and revered by her people, and her demigod husband all her life. A mother to nine children. *Nine*. Can you imagine?"

"I'd rather not," Eli chuckled, though he sobered when she lifted off of his chest, and sat back with her legs crossed to look at him with eyes as solemn as he'd ever seen them.

"Do you want children?" she asked.

"Doesn't really matter at this point," he said carefully, not wanting to examine the familiar pain lancing through him. "We've not been doing anything to prevent them."

Her hand flew to her womb, her features pensive. Perhaps troubled. "I suppose we should have discussed…"

"Do *you* want kids?" he countered.

She nodded, searching his features for something he didn't know how to give. "My parents were not what I'd call…happy. And, in the end, Emmett, Emmaline, and I were more of a secret burden to my father than a boon. He married my mother for love, but they were both destitute, so he stashed my mother away and married an heiress with a heart condition who wasn't expected to live a long life. Except she did, bearing him four more children. He ended up choosing his second wife over his first and kept us in a house in the country. We rarely saw him, and when we did, he wasn't kind. My mother withered without him, into a bitter old woman, with ironically poor health."

Plucking at an errant thread on the cuff of his shirt, she continued. "All my life, my siblings have been such a comfort to me, and finding the rest of my family has been wondrous. I've often dreamed of having children so I might lavish upon them the care and concern my parents never showed us. I plan to raise them to feel loved and wanted, because they would be. I'd like them to have siblings just as dear as mine, and more cousins than they can count to go on adventures with."

Eli knew her lovely fantasy to be just that. A fiction. A hope born of her youth and her loneliness that had the capacity to be crushed with the cruelties of fate.

"Rosaline," he started, taking her hands in his. "I lied to you."

She said nothing, gathering herself as if preparing for a terrible confession.

Maybe it was the stars. Perseus and Andromeda. Or the reality that he might have already planted a child inside of her. Something his soul yearned to do...

And yet.

"I told you I had no family," he began, a familiar pain blooming in his chest, guilt winching his ribs tight so his lungs couldn't fully inflate.

"You did. That your father and mother were both taken from you by the time you were ten."

"And they were...but what I didn't mention was that I had a younger brother at the time. Caleb."

Rather than berate him for the lie, her fingers curled around his. "Had?" She echoed the salient word with fathomless sympathy. "Past tense?"

Not far enough in the past, apparently. Not so long ago that he didn't still wear the pain on his skin. "When I was ten, he was just six. We were taken in by a mining family for a couple of years, and I promised to work so that I could send Caleb to school. He was born early and grew up on the scrawny side." Eli caressed his wife's knuckles, and turned her hands over to stroke at the smooth palms. His brother had soft hands...he'd been sensitive and anxious. Eli would have fought the entire world to protect him.

"Caleb had a head for books, so I kept working and he kept learning. When Morley invested in my mine a decade ago, I took some of that money and sent Caleb to college. He got a degree in mathematics. Learned all about accounting, finance, business, and trade. I'd struck gold by the time he graduated and made him my partner immediately. We'd this friend in Nevada, Beau, and he was our third musketeer. I made him foreman of many of my mines, and he became a very wealthy man in his own right."

The serenity he found in his wife's features blurred and disappeared as Eli stared into the past, plagued by every bitter emotion there was. "Beau and I always made a game of collecting things from digs and mines. Old things. Arrowheads, clay pottery, sometimes bones and fossils that had no business being in a desert. This game turned into a passion, and as men, we often financed archeological digs with preeminent universities, just to see what treasure was buried in the past."

He broke off. Wishing like hell the story ended there. He'd never spoken the words. Never told anyone of his loss, of the circumstances surrounding it and the reasons he had for keeping himself so tenaciously isolated.

"Like the treasure being catalogued and appraised over there?" Rosaline pointed to the corner where half of what he called the Midas Tomb waited in an organized chaos for the professor and the appraiser to return in the morning.

"Exactly like that, in fact." He sighed, scraping his hand over a stubbled jaw. "I've no idea who started calling me Midas, but Beau and Caleb thought it was hilarious that it caught on. In fact, they'd concocted a scheme to find the fabled Midas Tomb and hold the chalice his daughter drank from. The one that supposedly turned her to gold. The chalice was supposedly inlayed by a gem called the Anatolian Sapphire. Caleb found the sapphire through one of the digs in the Near East, and he paid a king's ransom for it."

"What happened?" she prompted, causing him to realize he'd fallen too quiet for too long.

"We were supposed to have come looking for the chalice together, Caleb, Beau, and I. But before we could look into it, something happened."

"Oh no." She held him tighter, pressing a kiss to his knuckles, correctly guessing the reveal of a corpse.

"There was a cave-in at one of the mines. A new acquisition, one I bought despite my reservations, on account of Caleb's nagging." The metallic tinge of that night's panic again threatened to choke him. The memory of digging until his hands bled. Of screaming Caleb's name. Of pulling his crushed body from the rubble.

And finding the bullet wound.

"Come to find out, Beau had been falsifying expense reports and buying cheap tools and safety gear. The beams were rotten. The chains bad. The working conditions...inhumane. He pocketed the savings." He'd realized that to ask why, was an exercise in futility. Greed was more powerful than just about anything, but... "How Beau could do that to other men, other miners, after throwing a pickaxe right next to me for almost fifteen years. And just as he was about to be caught, he took my brother with one well-placed bullet."

"My stars," Rosaline blinked, and a tear fell over the curve of her cheek and disappeared in the crease of her mouth. "Was this Beau found in the rubble, as well?"

"He'd swiped the Anatolian Sapphire and taken off. I hunted him all the way to San Francisco." Eli's heart hardened to that cold shard of granite it had been the day he confronted Caleb's murderer. The man he'd also called brother. "Know what his last words were to me before he was sentenced to hang?"

Rosaline shook her head.

"He told me Caleb had planned the entire thing. That

my brother was sore at me over some woman from three years prior who'd thrown him over for a shot with me."

Rosaline gasped, pressing her fingers to her lips. "And he never told you of his feelings for her?"

"Only after she and I—" He glanced up, realizing she'd gotten the gist. "But Caleb and I...we had it out about her. She wasn't someone I kept around, and I thought we'd buried the entire damned affair when I apologized. I told him a woman like that, who would pit brothers against one another and leave a good man like him for my fortune wasn't worth his time."

"And you'd be right," she granted.

"I guess he hated that he'd worked so hard to become an accomplished man, with an education and refinement, and I still was more successful than him. Five hundred thousand dollars was taken, and because I trusted both Beau and my brother, I didn't realize the extent of it until after they were both gone."

"Such an inconceivable amount of money," she breathed. "Did you recover it?"

"Yeah." Eli shrugged, his heart galloping after the same hot fury he'd felt at the betrayal. The same guilt. The same anguish. "It wasn't about the money, though. I'd have given it to Caleb if he'd asked. I'd given him every other damn thing. Worked my hands until they bled. I starved. Suffocated. Suffered beneath the ground...and he would plot against me...over a woman? I still don't believe it most days."

"He must have really loved her," she murmured. "I'm told love makes people do things that defy logic."

He snorted, bitterness still threatening to choke him. "Not me."

Her hands fell away from his as she reached for one of the kittens who'd toddled over, loudly demanding affection, her hair a curtain over her face when she said. "I suppose that made it difficult to trust people."

"It did," he said, curling his now empty fingers into a fist. "And everyone else made it impossible."

"Impossible?" she echoed. "How?"

"What do you imagine people wanted from King Midas?" he asked, no longer trying to keep the wrath from his voice.

She took longer than he expected to answer in a small voice. "Gold?"

Damn right. "I learned that family was most often the cause of violence. That the person you trusted the most had the easiest way to get to you. And my betrayal didn't end with family," he revealed, watching faces from his past float by with his lips lifted in a silent snarl.

"Lawyers embezzled from our trusts. Brokers undercut properties. Hell, I even found a couple of my lovers with a hand in my safe, or emptying my money clip when they thought I wasn't looking. The most recent was a bout with a woman I'd grown…fond of. I woke to an empty bed one night and found her in my office stealing plans and paperwork. She confessed a rival was paying her top dollar for something to sabotage me with. And I was the dupe who fell for it. For her."

"Everyone…takes from you." Her shoulders curled into themselves, as if she could somehow make herself smaller. "Steals from you."

He nodded. "I suppose it's why family has not been much of a happy ideal in my world. Why I made it to this age without a wife or children. Why I convinced myself that when a man has the kind of money I do, children will only wait for you to die to inherit it, anyhow. So why bother trying to have any?"

She nodded, and he wished he could see her face. That he could read what she was thinking. "Why do you continue to look for the Midas Tomb, when the search holds such bitterness for you?"

Eli puffed out his cheeks, tilting his heavy head back

to gaze up at the gilded darkness. "Because I finish what I start. I always have. And, I guess a part of me wants to hold that chalice. To get the Anatolian Sapphire back from whoever Beau sold it to. To have it as a reminder of something I'd lost sight of until now."

Reaching through the curtain of her hair, he cupped her chin and lifted it, ready to drown in the azure depths of her liquid eyes. "What's that?" she whispered through her tender tears.

"That Midas was able to break his curse. He got his daughter back before it was too late." Drawing her close, he kissed the salt of her grief from her cheeks. His sweet wife. Shedding tears for a loss that was not her own. Something soft bloomed inside of him, something as fragile as the first snowdrop peeking through the last of the winter freeze. Tendrils of hope, maybe. The beginning of a dream he'd abandoned long ago.

"Everyone takes and takes from me, Rosaline..."

She shuddered against him, and he drew her closer, cupping her head as her very nearness was like a balm on a raw wound.

"Everyone but you."

CHAPTER 10

Later that night, with a heart heavier than the arm her husband curled around her body, Rosaline snuck out of bed. After checking to make certain Eli remained sleeping, she crept through the darkness of Hespera House feeling just as furtive as she had the first time.

Though she and Eli shared a sleeping chamber, she'd the use of her own suite of accommodations, including a dressing room, receiving parlor, and washroom. Done in the colors of blond sand and turquoise, the rooms adjoined each other with arched and wide intricate doorways the same dark wood as the floors.

Padding into her dressing room on bare feet, Rosaline struggled to quietly move several heavy trunks of her things yet to be unpacked. These contained what she'd rather the servants not manage, such as keepsakes, diaries, a few documents, and, to her everlasting shame…

Her trove of plunder.

With adroit motions born of obsessive repetition, she extracted each one, lining them up like the monstrous little memories they represented.

Her first, a monogramed pen of her mother's, taken at age eleven, when Rosaline had asked her father to bring her back to London with him, and her mother had slapped her in front of everyone for her impertinence.

She'd not known at the time why her question distressed her family. The hurt and confusion had rippled through her with devastating physical discomfort. Nothing she tried alleviated it. Not counting her way up Fairhaven's many staircases. Not going through the house and turning on every single lamp. Not even reorganizing her wardrobe and all her cupboards, much to her maid's dismay.

When called back to her mother's parlor, this time to be punished for the lights, she'd fixated on the gleaming pen on the secretary. Staring at it had quieted her mother's shrill sanctions and presented a way to ease this untenable suffering.

When she'd swiped the pen and walked out without anyone noticing, an ever-present weight lifted from her chest, and whatever befuddling sensations coursed through her, diminished to a distant hum.

From her finishing school she'd taken exactly six things. The headmaster's pipe, Coreen McHugh's hair ribbon, Miss Danbury's sextant, a package of unidentified seeds from the gardener. And, to her chagrin, a small candle from the oratory. The owner of each item had done something to her, whether on purpose or not, to ignite that burning, stinging sensation and send it crawling across her flesh. She'd felt as if she'd a rash over her entire body. Not to mention the repetitive ringing in her ears, loud enough she couldn't believe others didn't hear it, as well. The thoughts and fears she couldn't escape, sometimes a whisper, other times a storm, screaming at her to take. Take. *Take.*

Anything.

Until she did.

Counting the older treasures as habit insisted she do, Rosaline reached into the wooden box where she kept her most recent acquisitions, and extracted what she'd been searching for.

A little bowl, no larger than a teacup dipped in metal she was beginning to fear was partly gold.

Marriage to Eli had been a miraculous turn of events, and the past weeks had been some of the happiest and most carefree in her life.

And yet, something about the event had triggered her horrid compulsion. She'd taken enough of his things that she'd had to dedicate an entire box to Eli.

This one full of happier memories, like the cufflinks he'd worn on their wedding day. One of his hair combs. A pearl-handled razor. Several bullets from his pistol. A gold paperweight. And a gilded letter opener with his name engraved upon it.

Elijah C. Wolfe.

He'd a middle name she didn't know.

They'd still so much to learn about each other... Even during the lovely conversations they'd shared over the past couple of weeks, she'd never learned of his tragedy until tonight.

He didn't know about this, her most horrendous flaw.

And he could never learn of it. Not only because it put her entire future in danger...

But because it would cause him pain.

All her life, Rosaline had done her best not to hurt anyone. Had tried to take things that were easily replaced, or not likely to be missed at all.

After the vulnerability Eli had trusted her with tonight, she'd done nothing but obsessively worry about this particular box. About him finding out just what sort of person he'd married.

And hating her for it.

She was going to return all of it, every last thing. Starting with the cup.

Furthermore, she was going to control herself. Even if

it seemed like she'd immolate from the inside out. Even if she never took another full breath. If her body shook with strain from now until her dying day.

For him, she would prevail over her own demon.

For *him*...she would do just about anything.

As she crept along the lush halls of Hespera House, Rosaline silently railed against the cruel twist of fate that would see her so happily married to a man so wounded by theft.

Her heart ached at the thought of his loneliness. And her soul had shriveled when he'd taken her in his arms and granted her the first little tendrils of his hard-won trust.

Her coarse American husband. Foul-mouthed and rough-skinned. His strong hands were capable of the utmost gentility. His caustic wit tempered to make her laugh. His hard lips kissed her with a tenderness she wasn't aware existed on this earth.

She loved the way he looked as if he didn't belong in his fine suits.

She loved the way he looked *at her*, with a mixture of possession, passion, and something deeper she didn't dare define.

She loved how his jaw never stayed smooth after a shave. And how his laugh sounded rusty, as if he'd not used it in a long time.

She loved the sparkle in his eye and the twitch in his right jaw when he was trying not to swear in front of her sisters.

She loved that he truly didn't give one whit about what people thought of him. That he respected no one and cared not for nobility nor ego, but insisted that people earn his good opinion, no matter their station.

She loved that he was compassionate to the working class, and even more so to the destitute. That he parted with his money more willingly than anyone she'd ever met. Gave to every charity who asked, dropped coin to ever beggar on the street. Purchased an entire cart full of blossoms so that the owner, who'd been suffering from a dreadful cold, could go home and rest.

She loved that he'd ordered the flowers delivered to every room in which she liked to linger.

The observatory most of all.

She loved him.

She loved Elijah Wolfe. Her husband. And she was going to do everything she could to demonstrate that love.

Slipping into the observatory, Rosaline made her way toward the tables used to catalogue the findings from the proposed Midas Tomb. The panes of the glass ceiling allowed in an anemic glow, and she calmed her nerves by counting each individual reflection on the floor as she tiptoed through them.

"One, two, three, fou—"

They disappeared as the lights flared to life, startling her so absolutely she lost her hold on the wooden box. It crashed to the floor with a splintering sound, the lid flying off and the contents spilling everywhere.

"Rosaline?" Eli's sleep-husked voice echoed through the observatory, fracturing her name into reverberating accusations as she squeezed her eyes shut in horror. "Are you all right? What are you doing in h—?"

With infinite slowness, Rosaline turned to find Eli stooping to retrieve one of the cufflinks from the ground with a bemused expression. "I thought I'd misplaced these… and…" He crossed to where his razor had slid to the rug her kittens had stained. Her heart didn't flutter with panic as she'd expected it to do. Instead, it shrank and skipped entire beats each time he found something else of his. Stopping altogether when he abandoned everything to a chaotic pile in order to use both hands to reverentially retrieve the cup.

"The set wasn't incomplete after all," he said as if to himself before finally skewering her with a look of dawning suspicion that quickly darkened with temper. "Tell me you didn't have this the entire time. That you didn't take it on the night we met and lie to me about it ever since."

Legs weak from trembling, Rosaline swallowed around a desert-dry lump in her throat and forced herself to meet his flinty dark eyes. "I can explain."

"You can *explain*." He threw his arms open in a sarcastic gesture, as if gathering an invisible audience to hear something more absurd than they'd ever believe. "Everyone *always* wants to explain *after* they get caught. Well, let's hear it, Mrs. Wolfe. Let's hear why *you* stole from me. Let's speculate as to why I would catch you with it the night I mentioned that people who were close to me had a remarkably predictable penchant of pulling this exact brand of bullshit."

"I heard what you've gone through, and it…it moved me, Eli. I have all of this because I was intent upon returning it to you." Bending her knees, she picked up his comb and held it out to him as a pathetic peace offering.

He simply stared at it, at her, as if the sight disgusted him. "Still doesn't explain why you took it all in the first place."

"I—I don't know why," she said, hating the tears that burned behind her nose. Hating how small her voice was becoming.

Hating herself most of all.

"I just…I just take things sometimes. I've done it always, and I can't seem to stop."

He made an ugly sound of disbelief, his lip pulled back in a snarl. "You can't stop?" he echoed, his voice rising in volume. "It's not that hard to not take things that don't belong to you, Rosaline. You just don't fucking do it."

She rushed toward him, beseeching him to listen, to

hear what she'd never had to say. "I don't take anything important. Nothing of value. I just...I can't help it. If I don't give in to the—"

"This had value to me." He brandished the cup at her. "This was priceless. Possibly one of the most valuable artifacts in the known world. I spent a bloody fortune on this. Ten fortunes. Above that, I sacrificed my freedom for it, as we'd never even be in this predicament if you'd not stolen it in the damn first place!" Whirling on his foot, he stalked to the tables, setting the cup next to a matching set. The ones inlaid with a ruby and an emerald.

She'd taken the chalice. The one belonging to the missing Anatolian Sapphire.

His words crushed her defenses, and she lost the battle with her tears. They leaked from a wound so deep, she worried that everything that gave her life would bleed away in the approaching storm of sadness.

Predicament? After what she'd thought was a rather happy beginning to their marriage, he still considered her a *predicament*? Still felt as though their match was a sacrifice of his beloved freedom?

Of course he did. She'd known that was what their arrangement was. That he'd been forced into the marriage by circumstance, Morley's coercion, and his own ambitions.

That it had been her doing.

And yet, she'd thought they'd somehow moved past that. That they'd established affection. Intimacy.

Perhaps more.

But no. To him she'd been a predicament, one he was trying to make the best of by at least enjoying her in bed.

"I knew it," he growled, spreading his palms on the table, the cup sitting between them. "I knew that night that you'd taken something, and I let those big, doe eyes of yours convince me otherwise." Pushing away from the table, he stalked toward the door, his stride long and angry.

"Eli," she sobbed his name, chasing after him. "Eli, wait."

He paused. Not turning back to face her but allowing his chin to touch his shoulder to cast her a sidelong look.

"I'm sorry, Eli. I—I thought this was harmless. Until you told me what you told me tonight... And I heard you, Eli. I vow it, I was putting everything back where it went. I'd made a pledge not to ever again touch what wasn't mine."

Exhaling for what felt like forever, he finally spoke in a quieter voice, though one as measured and cold as the underside of a glacier. "That's not nothing," he conceded. "But no more. No wife of mine will be a thief, you hear? I refuse to spend my life watching for you to slip up. Wondering what else you're going to take from me... I just..." Both fists curled at his sides. "I won't fucking do it."

The door slammed behind him like the gates of a fortress he'd erected between them.

The leaking dam behind her eyes burst, and she fell to her knees, wracked with sobs too powerful to deny. They tore through her, rending her strength obsolete.

This agony wasn't his fault.

It was hers.

How could he ever understand the weight of this demon?

CHAPTER 11

He'd left without her.

Rosaline haunted the halls of Hespera House for days, languishing like a ghost denied the paradise promised beyond this life.

The night she'd been caught, she mustered the courage to go back to their room, hoping she'd given him enough time to cool down. Finding their bed empty, she'd sat and waited for him to return…

And woke late the next morning, as alone as she'd ever been.

Rushing into the foyer, she'd noted her luggage was still piled neatly next to the door. Eli's, however, was gone. No goodbye. No note. No message left with the servants.

The trip was to have taken four days and three nights, and Rosaline decided that when Eli came home, he'd return to a different wife.

Her first order of business was to return everything as she'd vowed to do, arranging the pilfered items just so in the places she'd found them. Second, she sorted through the rest of her trove, and identified where and to whom each item initially belonged. It took a bit of doing, but she was able to post almost everything back to the original owner.

Anonymously, of course.

Tertiary, she threw every part of herself into the conquering of this dilemma, setting up a routine that eased her internal suffering. The thing about taking was, it resolved her misery for long periods of time. These rituals, the turning on of lights, counting the stairs, counting the brushstrokes in her hair and the seconds in which she cleaned her teeth. They allowed her to live without taking, but consumed so much of her time. So much of herself. And the internal pressure release was certainly more short-lived.

It didn't matter. It was how she'd cull her awful behavior.

Could she show this to him when he returned, this strategy she'd enacted? Did it make her seem more or less mad?

Perhaps he'd put her in an institution. It was what many husbands did when displeased by their wives.

And she'd actually deserve to be there.

Because her obsessive suffering was surely lunacy.

The idea filled her with so much terror, she doubled down on her diligence.

Emmett had been returned from one of those places a pale, sallow shadow of his former self. He refused to speak of what befell him there, but the bleak torment in his eyes when the subject was broached told her enough about what sort of hell it was.

Surely Eli had more compassion for his wife than to lock her away.

Perhaps not for a thief.

Because Rosaline couldn't face their bed alone, she spent her nights curled up on the sofa in the observatory, watching the winter sky.

Missing him.

It was a strange thing to love such a self-possessed and yet uncouth man. She couldn't predict from one moment to the next what societal rules he would revere, and which one's he'd ignore. He spoke his mind, and it was often both cutting and insightful. A cynic was her husband, but an amusing one. It was difficult to express the exact sense of satisfaction lent by the knowledge that such a toughened man held her in such tender regard.

She thought of how suddenly he'd fall asleep after their lovemaking, swift as a cat next to a fireplace after a bowl of cream. Rosaline would watch him slide from consciousness to slumber, going visibly lax, in awe of such an ability. His jaw, most often hard enough to chisel steel from stone would unclench, softening the tight line of his lips to a more sensuous curve. She found the dissonance wildly erotic.

How could she have only known him for three weeks and already feel as if a part of her was missing when they were separated?

Would she ever again get the chance to share his bed? His time?

His life?

She'd learned early that trust took years, sometimes a lifetime, to build and only one moment to break.

But she'd do it. She'd put in the years if that's what he required.

She waited in the front parlor the entire afternoon that they'd been scheduled to return from Devon, reading the same page of a book for hours without remembering a word.

Practicing the emphatic speech she'd prepared, she would sometimes get up to pace the floor, delivering the words for the kittens to critique. Then to the mirror until she was satisfied.

Then she'd try the book again, until the ticking of the wall clock threatened to drive her over the edge with its taunting.

When the last vestiges of daylight faded without a word or sign of his return, Rosaline snatched up her frockcoat and called over to Cresthaven.

Emmett and Emmaline were the only two alive who knew of her compulsive proclivity, and they'd had to dig within themselves for forgiveness when she'd taken some of their items in the past. They always treated her with sympathy, even though she didn't miss their worried glances at each other.

They forgave, but neither of them understood.

How could anyone?

Entering through the garden door, she found the house rather quiet, and followed the only sounds she could make out to the main parlor. There, Commander Carlton Morley, a knight of the realm and perhaps one of the most dignified and powerful men in the city, sat cross-legged on the rug arranging blocks with his year-old twins, Charlotte and Caroline.

Happening upon the tableau had bloomed an ache deep in her womb.

In her experience, Morley's only concession to indolence was rolling his sleeves to the elbows in the summer. But tonight, he'd abandoned his shoes and his vest, thrilling his twin daughters with silly smiles and rich laughter, those ice shards he had for eyes having melted into pools of brilliant love.

"Rosaline," he greeted warmly as she left the shadow of the doorway. "To what do I owe the pleasure?"

"I'm sorry to intrude. I was hoping to find Emmaline."

Picking up Caroline, he held her above his face as she squealed with glee. "I've been abandoned tonight, I'm afraid, as Emma and Pru took pity on Emmett and tagged along while Lucy dragged him to a lecture on lepidopterology, poor chap." Lowering his child, he made a rude noise against her belly, which caused her to squeal with glee. "Butterflies are boring. Aren't they, darling? Yes, they are. I'd much rather spend an evening with these beauties."

In reply to her father's adoration, Caroline sneezed into his open mouth.

Making a face, he set her next to her sister and wiped his features with a handkerchief. "Though I'll admit the society is a bit less sophisticated and quite likely to start randomly leaking from a myriad of places."

A yearning, yawning sadness banded around her ribs as she greeted her nieces with sloppy kisses and a stroke of each downy cheek. How blessed Prudence was in her match. Men rarely looked after their own children, leaving it largely to the mother or nannies.

What sort of father would Eli make? Heavy-handed like her own? Or soft-hearted like Morley?

"You've not heard from Eli, have you?" she queried with false tranquility. "He was supposed to return from Devon early this afternoon, and I've not heard from him yet. I was wondering if I should worry."

"I thought you'd gone with him to Devon, or I would have looked in on you." Morley sent her an apologetic look, and she wondered if anyone else had brothers as dear as hers.

"No need. I was feeling under the weather, so it was decided I should stay and rest. I'd not have made good company."

Morley nodded. "You do seem a bit pale, should I send for a doctor?"

"No, I'm much improved, thank you."

"I'm surprised Eli wouldn't stop at home to check on your well-being before taking himself off to Northwalk

Hall." His fair brows drew together in an expression of vague disapproval.

"What is at Northwalk Hall?"

"The antiquities auction, did he not mention?" He looked at her askance.

"I must have forgotten," she rushed. "I'm not familiar with Northwalk Hall."

"Well, the auction used to be elsewhere, but the manse was recently lost to a fire, so this year Dorian and Farrah Blackwell have offered to host it in their grand ballroom."

"I thought you were friends with Blackwell and the Countess Northwalk," she remembered.

A wry smile quirked at his ever-smooth jaw. "Apparently, several black-market figures will be in attendance, and so a man in my profession is not entirely welcome. Not that I much mind missing it. I'm in no mood for parties what with this wedding looming over us." Blinking away an errant frustration, he turned to give her his full attention.

"It surprises me Eli would attend an event with such people, given how…strong his feelings are regarding thieves."

His expression turned rueful as he locked his hands behind his back. "Well, he knows I spent my adolescence as a petty thief and still signed a contract with me. As far as Eli is concerned, business is business, and everyone is a crook. I think he only takes it personally, when it's personal."

"So I've gathered," she murmured.

"And this time, it's personal."

Her eyes searched his features, unable to cover her surprise. "It is?"

"Surely he's told you about how the Anatolian Sapphire was stolen from him by his business partner."

"He mentioned it."

"Well, rumor has it the gem will be on the premises."

Morley's mouth suddenly flattened to a grim line. "Now I'm wondering if Eli is there to confront the owner, dispute the provenance, or buy it for a second time at great expense. I hope it's the latter. Blackwell's men are notoriously dangerous." He turned to her, as if remembering he'd spoken out of turn. "Not to worry, though. Eli's as tough as a buffalo hide and he's one of the cleverest men I know when he cares to be. I shouldn't be worried at all."

Rosaline shook her head, trying not to let her despondency show. Eli would spend an evening with black market figures and notorious gangsters such as Dorian Blackwell, the Black Heart of Ben Moor. And yet, he could not stand her presence long enough for her to truly apologize.

When it came to his list of importance, she was understandably below a famous sapphire the size of a baby's fist.

"Anything I can do for you?" he offered. "Anything specific you are looking for?"

"No. Just in search of a sister, actually… Female complaints." She put a hand to her womb, hoping it sold the wrong message.

Morley's blush advertised that it had. "Oh, well, erm. Pru and Emmaline should be home in an hour or so, should I send them over?"

"That isn't necessary. Now that I remember where Eli has gone, I think I'm going to have an early night." Shoulders drooping with a heavy sigh, she picked up the corner of her skirt to turn and show herself out.

"Rosaline."

"Hmmm?"

She glanced back to find Morley regarding her with undue vigilance. "When I spoke with Eli at our last family dinner here, he was unlike I'd ever seen him. Content. Relaxed. Dare I say, happy. You are better for him than I could have ever imagined."

"I—I'm glad you think so." Rosaline did her best to swallow her anxiety. What would he say when Eli spoke to him next? How would she explain her theft to a man of the law?

"What about you?" he asked, uncurling himself from the floor to stand. "Marriage often favors the man and can be—unduly challenging for a woman. How is Eli treating you? Tell me he's behaving himself."

"He has been nothing but...deferential with me," she answered honestly.

"Glad to hear it." He relaxed into a winsome smile. "He's a good man, regardless of what he may claim. I know he's something of a philistine compared to the sort of society you're used to, but I hope you don't judge him too harshly for that."

Rosaline traced the grooves carved into the back of particularly ornate chair. "It's part of what endears him to me, actually. I find that in each other's company, it is easy to be...ourselves."

Or at least most of herself.

If only she could cut that one part out. If she could go to Titus Conleith and submit to his knife and be rid of her demon once and for all.

What she probably needed was an exorcist.

"Are you content with him? Fond of him?" Morley did his best to hide his particular interest in the matters of his friend and his sister-in-law, but he was terrible at doing so.

Rosaline flinched at the question, feeling as if she'd swallowed an entire hive of bees.

"I'm delighted with him."

"You don't look delighted," he noted with skepticism.

"I'm feeling poorly, is all. And...Eli has been gone a few days. I suppose I'm fighting a touch of melancholy."

He gave a grunt of commiseration. "I am a terrible grouse whenever Pru and I are parted too long. She is the keeper of my happiness, and takes it with her when she goes."

"That must be how I feel." Her smile was so brittle, she feared he could see right through it.

"It vexes me that he let you worry." Morley frowned. "That wasn't well done of him."

"Don't mention it to him," she requested, putting a beseeching hand on his arm. "He's not a man accustomed to marriage or family. It's made him remarkably independent, and I imagine that isn't an easy tendency to break."

Carlton patted her hand. "You're better than he deserves. I think he'll spend an entire lifetime realizing all the ways. I know I certainly do."

"Nonsense." Lifting on her tiptoes, she pressed a kiss to his sharp jaw, unable to help but notice the difference in aromas from her husband. The textures of their skin. The hues of their countenance.

She'd always secretly thought Morley was handsome, and hoped to have such a dignified, golden-haired husband someday.

Now, her preferences leaned in exactly the opposite direction. Her lips preferred a rough cheek to his smooth. A headier fragrance than his fresh one. And glinting dark eyes to his iridescent blue.

"Our entire family is unceasingly aware of how lucky we are to have you in our lives," she assured him. "Have a lovely evening with your girls."

"Get some rest, Rosaline." He led her to the door and opened it, ever the unfailing gentleman. "If you're not feeling better tomorrow, we'll have a doctor out to look at you."

"Thank you."

Rosaline fled back to Hespera House, calling for Hildie as she climbed the steps two at a time... She'd a golden ballgown she'd not yet worn, and Hildie had her in it and worked some magic with her hair in under an hour.

She couldn't go another night without seeing him. Without putting this thing between them to rest. One way or the other.

CHAPTER 12

Rosaline hadn't known what to expect, but it *certainly* wasn't her husband with another woman.

She'd done her best to stroll up to Northwalk Hall as if she belonged there, though she'd not been able to keep herself from staring up at the mansion that'd been built around one of London's oldest structures. Even the medieval buttresses had been worked into the breathtaking architecture, along with thoughtful, mischievous, and malevolent gargoyles perched on wide ledges to leer down at those converging on their lair.

After almost being turned away at the door for not having a printed invitation, she'd gained access when another guest had recognized her as Mrs. Wolfe, and told her where she could find her husband.

She found him, all right.

After threading through the ballroom, avoiding waltzing couples, a myriad of tempting trinkets, and several greetings from men hungry for an introduction, she finally spied him over by the gallery.

A searing lance of frigid ice pierced her heart, turning her extremities numb with cold, even in the close and overcrowded ballroom. Eli, looking like the devil's own deal broker, strode toward the gallery on the arm of a statuesque woman with a wealth of glorious dark hair and the bold features of a Greek goddess.

Indeed, the gods had been generous when crafting his companion, molding large, perfect breasts and remarkable hips that curved and indented dramatically to a lean waist. She'd an air of regal sensuality and the erect confidence of a woman who was aware of the eyes that followed her wherever she went. Her scarlet dress beset with rubies boasted a scandalous bodice that, in Rosaline's opinion, didn't deserve the designation, as it drew the eye to what it revealed rather than what it concealed.

Blinking a fog of disbelief from her vision, she recognized the woman as the Duchesse de la Coeur. Mercy and Felicity's dear friend who'd taken them around the world on her yacht. They'd only just returned for Emmett's wedding.

Rosaline had left Hespera House feeling more beautiful than she ever had in a dress that might as well have already been touched by King Midas himself.

But next to this temptress, she'd seem as dowdy as a church mouse.

Once they'd disappeared into the Northwalk gallery, she drifted closer to the door, stationing herself next to one of the hip-tall vases overflowing with breathtaking flower and flora arrangements that bracketed the entry.

Peering around her ostentatious hiding place, she was dismayed to have lost them altogether. How was that possible? The only other exit to the gallery was on the other side of the room, and there was no physically viable way for them to have reached the door in time to avoid her. A few other couples meandered about the palatial room, but all of them did so, it seemed, in order to whisper to each other without being overheard.

"You are going to have to tell me your price for this information, Duchesse. Whatever it is, I'll pay double."

Eli's deep, unmistakable twang reverberated from just on the other side of the door, around which Rosaline hadn't been able to see without being a little too obvious.

"I've no need for your money, Mr. Wolfe."

Of course Eli would take up with a French Duchesse possessed of a voice made for sin. What man wouldn't?

"You must let me repay you," Eli insisted. "I've been after the Anatolian Sapphire since it was taken from me six years ago. It belongs in a set I've uncovered from where they believe the Phrygian King Midas was buried near the River Lydia in Assyria. The sapphire is said to have been parted from the Midas Chalice before it was buried with the king, which means I could be the first man to reunite the gem with its intended setting. Such an opportunity is priceless."

The Duchesse's laugh was husky, tinged with an implicit salacious suggestion. "What an intriguing offer, Monsieur Wolfe. I'm certain I'll be able to think of something, eventually. Indeed, it's never a bad thing to have a man such as you owe me a favor, *N'est-ce pas*?"

"Very few can claim to do so," he replied, his voice as velvety as she'd ever heard it. "But I'm a man who always repays his debts...with interest."

Rosaline held her breath, swallowing the sob climbing up her throat. He'd used that voice of his to set her loins on fire. To soothe her anxieties and to release her inhibitions. It was as dark and graveled as a moonlight quarry, and the Duchesse was not immune to its effects.

Did this mean she'd lost her husband's affection and regard completely? Was she eavesdropping on him courting his new intended mistress?

She wouldn't blame him; the woman *was* breathtaking, closer to his age, and obviously full of the self-confidence and sensual know-how Rosaline lacked.

Not to mention, she'd had a hand in returning a valuable gem that had been stolen from him...

Whereas Rosaline was a thief who'd broken his trust.

Swirling gowns blurred into a kaleidoscope of color interrupted by the black lines of men in their evening finery spinning butterflies on the ballroom floor.

She would not cry in public. She would *not*.

"So, tell me, Monsieur Wolfe, how do you plan on retrieving the Anatolian Sapphire?" the Duchesse queried. "It is not up for auction tonight and will only be on display here in the gallery for a short time. Surely you don't intend to steal it."

"I intend to get it back by any means fair or foul," her husband answered in a voice reenforced by iron. "Can't steal what is already yours. And I have the documentation to prove ownership right here."

"The sapphire has exchanged hands many times on the black market, where provenance is often as false as the treasure," the Duchesse warned. "Whoever owns it now, is linked to the infamous Black Heart of Ben More...to cross him is to cross death. The room it is being held in is on the very top floor and is guarded by men who are—how do you say?—armed to the teeth. It is a dangerous thing you are considering."

"I'm a dangerous man," Eli stated as if it were bloody obvious. "And this...*this* is a risk worth taking. I don't care who the owner is. I will fight him in this house. I'll fight him in court. Hell, I'll have a stand-off in the fucking town square if that's what he wants, I'll shoot him in the eye at ten paces. But I'm walking away with that sapphire, and I don't mind stepping over his body if I have to."

"I will never understand men," the Duchesse sighed. "This lust you have for such things. Rocks that are made valuable only because someone assigned them value so long ago, we cannot remember why. What is a sapphire? Nothing but a blue stone. Nothing to be killed over, surely."

"Says the woman draped in rubies," Eli teased.

"Touché, Monsieur." That husky laugh again. "But if someone were to take these from me, I would not put myself in harm's way to get them back. As you can see, I don't need rubies in order to sparkle."

Eli's chuckle was warm and fond. "No, ma'am. No, you do not."

Rosaline imagined the woman touching Eli's arm. Brushing her décolletage against him in that outrageously flirty way the French had.

She wanted to claw the Duchesse's eyes out. Yearned to storm in there and drag her husband home by the ear and—and *what* exactly? She couldn't force him be loyal to her. Couldn't coerce him into forgiving her any more than she could compel him love her.

So…what did she do now?

The chalice she'd taken had an empty slot, which was why she'd thought it lacked value.

But it'd been the only thing in the trove he'd truly desired.

Lord, what a mess she'd made of things. And now, Eli was about to attempt a deal with some of the most ruthless men in the underworld and the powerful nobles with whom they did business.

"The auction doesn't begin for half an hour hence," the Duchesse said. "Shall we dance while we wait?"

"Afraid not." Rosaline didn't have to be looking at her husband to see the little divot of chagrin that would appear in his left cheek when he was being self-effacing. "I never learnt to waltz. Too busy busting rock or amassing a fortune."

"Perhaps your new wife could teach you?"

Rosaline couldn't tell if the Duchesse was being cruel or not…if they were laughing at her.

"How about you point me in the direction of the man who owns my sapphire, Duchesse? I'd love to meet him. To get a measure of him."

He was avoiding the subject of his wife. God, she wished that didn't hurt so much.

"I warn you, he's a loutish boor. He'll wax poetic about his appalling exploits in Egypt to anyone who will listen."

Eli made a disgusted noise. "I dislike it when people wax anything. Not poetic. Not prophetic. And not philosophical."

Rosaline turned away as the Duchesse's amused laugh sounded closer than before. She ducked around a corner as they reached the door from the gallery to the ballroom and watched them stroll away toward the solarium where rows of chairs were set before a podium. Eli's broad back and strong arms created the perfect bulwark for the endlessly elegant Duchesse.

She didn't know if she were being bold, or just reckless, but Rosaline followed them for a moment, daring him to turn around. To find her.

To know she'd found them.

"That surprises me, monsieur," the Duchesse was saying. "You strike me as a man of surprising depths and profound philosophies."

"Nah." Eli's arm lifted to swipe at the back of his neck, smoothing the fine hairs there. "In my philosophy, we are just meat, bone, and blood collecting shiny things to slake our bottomless hunger before we die."

"How sad, that you feel this way." The Duchesse looked over at him, true pity softening her gaze.

"It's not so sad," he replied. "Not for a man like me, who is about to get his shiny rock back and put it with all my other shiny things. My collection is bigger than most, therefore I must be satisfied with the life I have." His words were dry enough to make the Sahara seem tropical.

"I fear you will find these so-called shiny things cold and meaningless once you procure them," the Duchesse cautioned sagely. "The joy of their acquisition will be short-lived and ultimately empty."

"That may be...but there's been a voice in my head for six years, screaming at me to hunt it down. Keeps me up nights. Interrupts any moment of peace I might carve out for myself. And I need to silence it for good."

The Duchesse gave him a searching look from beneath her lashes, and Rosaline wondered if he'd confided in her about his brother, Caleb. Or if she were just a very perceptive woman.

"As you say." She dipped her chin in a nod of deference.

Rosaline couldn't take another step, and she stood in the middle of the spectating crowd encircling the ballroom dance floor, watching as people parted before the stately-looking couple.

This was what he'd come to England for. The Midas Chalice and the Anatolian Sapphire.

He'd go to war to obtain it, in order to quiet the memory of his brother's screams.

Chewing on her lip, Rosaline felt a familiar vibration slither through her, tightening her belly with a sickening dread.

The need.

Sometimes it was a wicked whisper, easily ignored. This time it was a roaring tempest, churning her blood into froth. Pricking her skin with the bites of a thousand driving shards of ice. Threatening to sweep her away and carry her to some dark nether where she'd drown in her despair and be forgotten to those depths by all those she loved.

And suddenly, she knew what to do.

Lifting the hem of her skirt, she made an abrupt about-face on her heel and marched toward the grand staircase. Calling upon years of experience, she hid her turmoil behind a mask of serenity, smiling at the people she passed as she climbed.

Finding herself at the top of the fourth-floor steps, she came face-to-face with a huge, bald man standing sentinel in front of a red velvet rope that stated "Private."

"Oh," she stumbled a bit, and righted herself on the banister. "Hello."

"You're not to be here, miss," he said in a gruff Northumberland brogue. "Go back down with the other guests and wait your turn for a peek at the goods."

"Ever so sorry," she simpered, sidling up to the man who seemed fascinated by the fit of her frock. "I'm actually supposed to meet someone up there," she improvised. "I'm...to model one of the necklaces on auction."

His nonexistent eyebrow lifted as he inspected her chest, naked of any adornment. "A model, you say? I wasn't told about ya."

"Were you not instructed to let me by for the fitting?" she asked. "I apologize for the oversight, Mr..."

"Peckering." He smiled wide enough for her to notice a few of his back teeth were missing.

"Mr. Peckering. You are an absolute gem for executing your vocation with such diligence. How about I simply go and fetch the lady of the house so she can clear this up—"

"No need." He put his hand out to stop her, and she grimaced when his fingers cinched around her upper arm. "I'm not keen to interrupt the Black Heart of Ben More's wife. You can pass. Just be quick about your business." He unhooked the rope and pulled it aside, allowing her access to the shadowy hall beyond.

"Thank you, Mr. Peckering."

It took every bit of starch in Rosaline's knees to walk down the hall as if she were supposed to be there, especially since she could feel the sinister guard's eyes on her the entire way.

Flustered, she rounded the first corner she could find,

and took a moment to orient herself. The passages of Northwalk Hall were long and lined with several doors. She wandered down this one feeling overwhelmed by choice and pressed for time.

Peering around a corner, she spied four men standing guard outside of a double-doored chamber at the end of the next hall. They'd strange bulges in their suit jackets that she had to imagine were the weapons Duchesse de la Coeur referred to.

Doing a few quick calculations, Rosaline was fairly certain that door faced north, so its windows would be on the east side of the manse. Which meant...

Turning behind her, she tried a door latch and sighed with relief when it opened. Though the door was just as wide as the others, she'd stumbled upon a linen closet deep enough to fit three servants, complete with a table for ironing and a window no person could possibly fit through close to the ceiling. Only used for venting the space to prevent and mold, she surmised.

Trying the next door, she found a tidy bedroom surely used for visiting valets or ladies' maids who served important guests. The accommodations were certainly nicer than servant's quarters, but not grand enough for guests of the master and mistress of the house.

Shutting herself in and bolting the door, Rosaline was relieved to find that the window latch was very similar to so many in this part of London. Easily unlocked from the outside with something like...*This.*

Swiping a letter opener from the secretary, she went to the window, depressed the latch, and leaned out to check the width of the ledge.

Easily doable, though it would take some finesse to circumvent the gargoyle at the corner.

Looking back at the door, she indulged in one of Eli's favorite curse words as she committed to the task.

She'd get Eli his sapphire by putting to use the dubious skill she'd mastered over the years.

She wanted to gift him the peace he sought, without him having to suffer recriminations.

Stepping out of her heavy skirt, she tied her petticoats between her legs, making a rather poufy pair of pantaloons out of them. Scooting up on the windowsill was easier than expected and from there she simply swung her legs around and slid down to the ledge.

It would take some doing to lift back up, but that was a problem for her future self to solve.

The night was just about moonless, and the illumination of such an incredible gathering was kept to the first and second floors, leaving the top of the house secured in shadow, for the most part.

Heights were not counted among Rosaline's many anxieties, so she flew on featherlight feet along the ledge, until she reached a stone monster perched on the corner pulling a dreadful face.

"Pardon me," she whispered, taking hold of his goblin-like ears in order to throw one leg around his perch and wriggle around to find stable purchase before scooting her back leg along. "I'll only have to do this once more," she informed him apologetically. "Please don't tell my husband I straddled you. He's not a forgiving sort."

Now was an odd time for levity, but sometimes a burst of humor would appear at the most stressful of moments.

Finding herself safely on the other side, she peered into a darkened window, surmising that each room on this side would have at least two, if this bedroom was any indication. The guarded door had been four counts down the hallway, so she hurried past eight windows, ducking beneath the lone glowing one—number five.

Taking a breath, she carefully peeked over the window ledge to find a darkened room stacked with open cases.

She was making a distressing habit of this, breaking into the treasure troves of her wealthy peers. Finding the scant moments when their plunder wasn't hidden away in a vault, but behind a window too high to be opened from the outside over a ledge too thin for most everyone but herself.

This time, she wasn't taking for herself. That had to mean something, hadn't it?

The latch didn't spring as easily as the ones at Hespera House, but she managed after a bit of a struggle with the letter opener to lift it from the hitch and swing the window outward. Boosting herself into the window was the most difficult thing, but she managed to do so quietly...if inelegantly.

Standing up, she dusted herself off, hoping her simple gold bodice hadn't been too damaged in the struggle with the ledge. It was impossible to tell in the dark.

Inching carefully around the room only lit by the ambient London night, she found a lamp and placed it as far as she could from the door, so as not to illustrate illumination from underneath.

Lighting it, she turned the wick as low as possible before starting her search of the room.

It was a lesson in opulence. A plunder only deserving of the greatest pirate, or king, or even a dragon.

Stunning paintings were carefully placed next to priceless art and sculpture. Some of them considered fabled, were they not tangible in this very room. Necklaces belonging to beheaded queens. Canvases painted by masters long thought lost to war. Bejeweled weapons. Ancient pottery, tools, and trinkets. Weapons encrusted with jewels. The crown jewels of forgotten empires winking like fallen stars.

Rosaline touched none of it, though she quite literally ached to do so. This room was akin to a museum, and her greatest wish would be to study every last artifact.

Alas, time was of the essence.

Leaving anything in a display case after a cursory perusal, she began to open traveling trunks and boxes full of soft batting or shreds of wood and paper. Most she found empty. Until…

A leather satchel with an odd padlock on it had been abandoned by itself in a cupboard. Slicing through the straps with a whispered apology to the owner, she opened it and pulled out the kind of purse used for coins some hundred years past. More a pouch than anything.

Pulling at the strings, she reached inside and extracted something covered in a velvet cloth.

Rosaline held her breath as she unwrapped an uncut sapphire half the size of her palm. Wait, no, upon closer inspection she realized it had been shaped somewhat. Not into the precise, reflective gems they made these days, but in a way one might expect a jeweler with only rudimentary tools to have cut it.

This had to be it. The Anatolian Sapphire. It matched the gems in the other cups she'd spied in Eli's collection, and she'd stake her life that if she placed it against the prongs on the chalice, it'd be a perfect fit.

Heavy bootsteps vibrated the ground beneath her, so she lifted her petticoats and shoved the sapphire into a pocket sewn into her drawers before re-knotting the hem between her legs.

Diving through the window, she slid onto the ledge and closed the panes just as the latch to the door depressed and a seam of light from the hallway sliced at the carpet.

Rosaline ducked, flattening herself against the ledge and the wall in a ghastly uncomfortable crouch.

"No one's in 'ere," rasped a man who was either quite timeworn or an avid smoker. "Wot did you say she looked like?"

"Young. Pretty. Little. Brown hair and big blue eyes. Wore a yellow dress. Said she was a model for tonight."

"Well, she inn't," the older voice interjected. "Like I said, there's no models tonight."

"Strange," Peckering muttered. "Anything missing in 'ere?"

"Nah. Not that I can tell. And the boys said they've seen and 'eard nothing."

"You leave this lantern on?"

"No. You?"

"No."

"You search the rooms?"

"'Ere on the fourth floor, yeah."

"Well, get to searching the other floors, then. Take a few men with you."

Rosaline breathed a sigh of relief when they slammed out of the room, and quickly made her way back toward the valet room.

Apologizing for, yet again, molesting the gargoyle, she shimmied back into the window, her limbs much less strong and steady than before.

That was close. Too close.

And Peckering knew what she looked like…

Rosaline stepped back into her skirts, securing them beneath her bodice and smoothing her hands down her thighs. In the mirror on the wash basin, she fixed a few tendrils of hair that'd escaped her coiffure, while she planned what to do next.

If they'd all gone to the third floor, she could slip toward the servant's stairs and let herself out through the staff entrance on the lower floor.

It was her greatest hope of escape without being recognized, by Peckering, Eli, or the few peers with whom she was acquainted.

She'd present Eli with the sapphire just as soon as he returned home to her…

If he ever did.

Carefully letting herself into the hall, she kept an eye out for guards and guests alike as she made her way toward the south servant's stairs. Finding the door, she wrenched it open and dove inside, closing it against the long hall in which she'd felt so vulnerable.

Thank God, her luck had not given out. She was alone in the stairwell, at least for a couple of floors.

When she'd reached the second landing, the doors to the lower story burst open, and a battalion of black-garbed servants spilled through. "I don't have to remind you to handle everything as if it was more important than your own children…they're certainly more valuable," barked whoever was in charge. "We'll arrange in order of presentation behind the curtain to the left of the podium."

The veritable army marched up the stairs to the boss's cadence, some of them murmuring in excitement to themselves.

Blast, they were on their way to the fourth floor to collect the valuables for auction. By the time the Anatolian Sapphire was found to be missing, she'd best be missing as well, if she hoped to escape.

Left with little choice, Rosaline dove through the doors that let her onto the second-floor hall.

And straight into the arms of a leering Mr. Peckering and his smokey-voiced compatriot.

"Gotcha," he growled in triumph as he seized her with arms as large and marbled as a slab of fatted beef. He'd imprisoned his arms to her sides, lifting her off her feet against the curve of his paunch.

"Wait!" she gasped, struggling for breath against his crushing hold. "Put me down!"

"Not until me and Hector, here, ask you a few questions," he snarled. "The first of which is why you lied to get past the rope."

Hector was a mixture of what she'd expected. A wiry

man who was younger than he sounded, but plagued with the leathery skin and rheumy eyes of a man doomed to die with a pipe in his teeth.

Rosaline struggled like an ensnared bunny against the burly brute as he dragged her into a doorway held open by his friend. "You're going to suffer for this," she warned. "I'm the sister of the Baron of—"

"As if I'm going to believe anyone you claim to be," he snorted, turning on the lights to a cozy sitting room before setting her down hard on a soft chair.

"You don't understand!" she cried. "My husband is—"

"Your 'usband inn't 'ere," Hector rumbled.

"Listen," she laced her fingers in front of the two towering men like a penitent in prayer. "I...I've been unfaithful to my husband. Here in this house, in one of the bedrooms on the top floor. And—I left something behind. That is why I was dishonest with you. I had to retrieve it before it was discovered." With her heart galloping at the pace of an entire stampeding herd of wild horses, and her legs trembling from the strain of her venture and the shock of her capture, it wasn't difficult to summon a few tears to lend her story credibility.

"I beseech you to have mercy on me," she begged. "I meant no disrespect to your duties, but you don't know what will be done to me if my sin is revealed."

Hector ran his hand over a hairline fast receding and winked over at Peckering. "You were right, she's a pretty little thing, inn't she?"

She yearned to inform them that she wasn't a thing, she was a woman. A person. Someone worth their compassion...if they had any.

Peckering sized her up with one wide eye. "I'm feeling downright merciful today, wouldn't you agree, Hector?"

The other revealed teeth in desperate need of a good cleaning. "Merciful. Indeed."

"Here's wot we'll do... We'll keep our mouths shut

about finding you where you ought not be, if you repay us with the favor of your own mouth."

Rosaline blinked several times, a lead weight landing in her gut. Surely they weren't blackmailing her for—

Hector's hands went to the waistband of his trousers, erasing all denial in regard to what they were demanding of her.

"I can't," she said, springing to her feet and diving around a leering Peckering. She made it as far as the door latch, gripping it before a hand seized her hair and yanked hard enough to rip her head from her neck.

A desperate word escaped on a sob, both an invocation and an appeal for help.

Eli.

CHAPTER 13

Eli didn't recognize the man whose teeth went flying out of his face. Didn't care to. The motherfucker put his hands on Rosaline.

And in doing so, forfeited his life.

Simple as that.

The bone of his jaw shattered with a *thoroughly* satisfying crunch, and the tub of guts and gore crumpled to the ground, too unconscious to catch his weight with anything but his ruined face.

Next came his hatchet-faced friend, who'd reached into his jacket to pull a pistol out of the shoulder holster.

Eli beat him to it, wrenching the gun from the man's grip, spinning it on his itching trigger finger, and whipping him across the temple with the butt of the weapon, hard enough to leave a significant dent in his skull.

Having dropped them both, he spun the weapon back and pointed the barrel at the fat man's head. "Tell me," he snarled, his lips barely able to form the words. "They hurt you? I'll end them."

He couldn't look at her. Couldn't face a telling pain in her eyes without ripping the men's bones from their sockets with his bare hands.

Eli had always considered his temper to have a

medium to long fuse, depending on the situation. Once ignited he blew hot as a smith's forge.

But this...this cold, hard, eerie demon inside of him was something new. It licked at his bones with a numb sort of calm, locking him down with a fury so intense, it coalesced into a strange implosion of pure, white rage.

The violence running through him wasn't primal or feral as it had been in the past, as he expected to be when it came to her.

It was a lethal calculation. A precise and fanatic joy at the thought of carving the flesh that'd profaned her away, from the man's meat and making him watch.

"Nothing happened," she said shakily. "Not yet..."

"Good." He cocked the pistol.

"Wait! Stop!" She lunged forward, and Eli instantly released the hammer, respecting the weapon enough not to want it anywhere near his wife. "You'll bring the entire house if you shoot."

Frantic little fingers tugged at his sleeve, and permeated the ringing of rage in his ears.

Eli's head swiveled on a neck stiff with the bristle of a beast about to strike, his eyes finding the woman at his side.

His woman. His wife.

Mine.

Language still eluded him, somewhat, and would probably do so until he had Rosaline alone and could assess her state of well-being for himself.

Seizing her by the elbow, he half led, half dragged her from the room and into the long corridor, leaving those sacks of ripe shit to become someone else's problem.

To his surprise, his wife trotted meekly beside him, in fact, she clung to his arm as if it were the only solid thing keeping her from dropping off a steep precipice.

The sound of a household in a state of alarm arose with a swift and astonishing ferocity. Running steps pounded above their heads and along the stairs, chaos erupting below them. Panicked calls and barked commands converged from all directions.

With a little *eep* of shock, Rosaline took the reins like a tugboat pulling a steamship, leaning all her weight into the task until they'd reached a door that she yanked open and shoved them both inside.

Eli stood stock-still, allowing his eyes to adjust to the dimness of some sort of linen closet. He allowed lungs full of honeysuckle to anchor him back into reality.

All night he'd been plagued with this electric prickle of awareness, this low vibration in his body that seemed attuned only to her presence. Several times, he looked for her, and several times he'd called himself nine kinds of idiot.

Until a flash of gold caught his eye, and he whirled to watch a woman—his woman—racing up the main flight of stairs. She'd been too far to see her face, but Eli knew how Rosaline moved, had studied the shape of her limbs and the effortless grace of her walk for weeks now. He'd memorized every curve and hollow, and how her skin looked in all shades of light and dark.

Once he'd extracted himself from his conversation and maneuvered to the staircase, she'd disappeared. So, he'd all but torn Northwalk Hall apart searching for her.

And was so damned glad he did.

Because the thought of those brutes pawing at her...of that desperate way she'd gasped his name when he'd gone to investigate the noises behind that door...

Eli felt the evil chill of retribution rising in him again. What if he'd not been there when she needed?

"What the everlasting fuck are you doing here, Rosaline?" he demanded in a voice that he knew damn good and well rendered their hiding place obsolete. "You could have been—"

Her body collided with his only for both of her hands to clamp over his mouth. "They'll hear you."

"Then answer my question," he remonstrated in a throaty whisper muffled behind the pressure of her fingers. He had the strangest urge to suck them into his mouth. To bite and nip them. To throw her over the first thing he could find and fuck away some of this cold dread.

Goddamn but his blood was up. He needed to calm the hell down, and being locked in a small space with the lithe body he'd missed with a visceral misery was doing exactly nothing to help.

"I was looking for the husband who'd been missing for *days*." Her whisper was enunciated with an angry fervency that matched his own. "I knew you were due to arrive today, and when you didn't come home, I went to find you."

He brushed her hands aside, wishing his lips didn't taste like her skin. That the slight flavor she'd left there didn't produce a roaring hunger in his gut, and lower. "Who told you I'd— Oh. Right. Fucking Morley."

"Don't blame Morley," she hissed in a voice more acidic than he'd ever heard from her. "He wrongly assumed I'd accompany you to such events as your *wife*. I came to make amends, so you can imagine my surprise when I found you'd trotted a continental trollop out as your show pony."

"Trotted...a what?" He paused, staring down at what he could make out of her shadow, trying to figure out what the hell nonsense she was spewing. "Hold on here, woman, the only one who has cause to be angry is me. You don't get to show up here uninvited, ruin my plans, and get yourself locked in a room with those fuckwits who might have—"

"I didn't 'get myself' anywhere. They grabbed me from the hall and forced me into that parlor."

The picture that invoked in his head brought him to the very breaking point of his sanity. "What the hell were you doing up there alone in the first place? Were you casing the place for something to take?"

Apparently, she had better eyesight in the dark because her slap landed exactly where it ought to on his cheek. "You can go to hell." Her voice cracked on a perilous note.

"Always assumed I would," he bit back, the hot sting of her slap sending a shower of sparks surging all the way down to his cock.

"And take your mistress with you, you...you perfidious, supercilious *cur*!"

Eli rocked back a little, stymied by her adorable stab at insults. If he ever found out what she called him, he'd surely be offended. But for now, he couldn't help the little tug of amusement at the corner of his lip. "You're jealous?"

"I'm livid!" She pushed at his chest, practically bouncing off of it. He wished he could see the sparks in her eyes, could watch her snap and snarl like a little lap dog finding the rage of his wolfish ancestors.

Probably she was the prettiest angry thing in the wide world.

No.

This time he stopped short of slapping his own self.

No. Now wasn't the time to go soft. He was angry with her. Betrayed by her. She was the embodiment of what he detested most in this world. A thief. A liar. Someone he couldn't trust as far as he could—well, maybe that analogy wouldn't work... He could probably throw her pretty far.

"You think I'm taking up with the Duchesse? There's nothing between her and me but friendly business."

"I heard you two in the gallery," she spat. "Cooing at each other like two mated doves. You paraded her around this grand house in front of all these important people like a peacock, while I sat at home alone, waiting for you to walk in the door so I could prostrate myself before your mercy, and beg you on my knees for forgiveness." The fury in her voice wobbled, filling with the tight threat of tears that tugged at a heart not ready to forget who she was. What she was.

What she'd done.

His blood surged once again, but he was too hot to identify the emotion. Rage? Pain? Lust? Some startling amalgamation of all three?

"Then do it," he said, a dark intent threading through his veins.

She stilled. "What?"

"Get on your knees, little wife." His cock flexed and jerked at the images those words provoked. "Beg my forgiveness."

"No," came the steely reply. "You've your French whore for that. I changed my mind the moment I saw your heads together."

Infuriated. Inflamed. He seized her shoulders and hauled her against him, crushing his lips to hers.

Sweet fuck, he'd missed this.

Missed *her*. Three nights without her had turned him into something like a pathetic hound, both hating and adoring the mistress that'd beaten him. He hated her and burned for her. Tossed around knotted sheets like a restless addict denied his opiate, wishing he'd forget her like he had so many other women. That she hadn't burrowed into his heart like a tick…all the while intending to suck him dry.

In his weakest moments, he'd even convinced himself it wouldn't be so bad. He'd all the wealth in the world, and had intended to share it with her from the beginning. If that were the case, had she really stolen from him at all?

Then he remembered how it felt to pull his brother

from the rubble. To look the man he'd trusted the most in the eye, and see all the deviant emotions he'd missed before. The greed and the resentment. The victory in his pain. The torment of a seed planted he'd never be able to confirm or deny.

Never again, he'd vowed. Never would he allow himself to trust.

And the woman in his arms had proven that very pledge a smart one.

Breaking the kiss, he looked down at her, catching a faint gleam off the whites of her eyes. "I couldn't fuck the Duchesse if I wanted to," he said, his grip tightening when he felt her tense, unwilling to allow her any distance. "But I don't, goddammit. There are a lot of beautiful women in the world, Rosaline, and I could buy most of them regardless of how I look. But what sticks in my craw the most, is that I can't look at a single fucking one of them without thinking of how she isn't you."

She put her hands against his chest but didn't push him away.

"I don't think it matters how angry I ever get with you, woman, I'll come crawling when you crook your finger. Because no one else makes me this hard. No one else could have me so spitting mad, so close to getting my hands on the one thing I came to this frigid country to obtain, and here I am in a fucking closet for some reason, ready to sacrifice everything for one more chance to be inside you."

She met his next kiss with an explosive, confident response he'd not expected.

Her lips were full pillows of pleasure, her mouth smooth and hot, slippery and succulent. Her tongue sparred with his, matching him thrust for wet, velvet thrust. Each stroke sent dizzying, delirious sensations spiraling through him, whipping him into such a frenzy, he was certain he'd lost his mind.

And was in danger of losing even more to this confounding woman.

If only he could make himself cold enough. Hard enough. Craft a heart of steel and stone to keep her out. To lock it in a glacier at the top of the world. Somewhere her inviting warmth couldn't tempt him away from himself.

Because she did. That icy wrath that'd overcome him earlier had miraculously melted before the inferno he found in the slick heat of her mouth. He was flooded with liquid fire. Boiled in days of lonely yearning. Lost to a tempestuous firestorm of possession and anger and fear and...and something he couldn't allow himself to define.

In her arms, he forgot. Forgot the load of his loss and the cut of betrayal.

Even hers.

Eli's hands roamed her, gripped at her arms, her hips, her ass, letting her feel the true strength of his hands for the first time.

Rather than shrink from his untampered power, she surged against him with a harsh sound ripping from her throat.

For a moment he'd realized, not for the first time, how easily she'd break. How small her bones were.

How could someone so damned fragile possess the power to destroy him?

The thought was sobering enough to stop him. If she'd wanted to, she'd have been able to pull away. To run.

But she chose that moment to score her nails down the front of his shirt, and in doing so, she untethered the last of his control from this beast of lust he'd become.

The one with teeth and claws.

Cupping her neck, he kissed her hard. Dominating her with his mouth. Fucking her with his tongue.

Warning her what was about to happen.

Threading his fingers in her hair, he curled them into

a fist, imprisoning her head as he rotated her away from him and bent her over the outline of an ironing table.

A whimper escaped her when he nudged her feet apart with his own.

But she made no move to stop him.

Tossing her skirts above her waist, he ignored a soft gasp as he rent her drawers in half and discarded them at her feet.

It was a bittersweet hell not being able to see her bent for him like this. He could imagine the pouty lips of her pussy splayed beneath the soft curve of her ass and the sight would probably have made him come in his own hand.

He found the smooth curve of her hip in the darkness, traced the cleft of her ass down to find the slit that instantly drenched his hand with desire.

He relieved himself from his own trousers, and drove into her with one savage thrust, branding her with the iron heat of his need, not stopping until he'd ground the bones of his hip against her.

Home. He gasped out a hard breath of relief.

She made a sound he couldn't identify, her feminine muscles clenching against his intrusion like a velvet fist.

Even in the red haze of his fervor, he was able to still. To seat himself deep within her and soak in the sensation of just being there. Waiting for her soft, tight core to give way to his intrusion.

Sweat bloomed beneath his suit and against his hairline. His teeth clenched. Muscles bulged. After a few pulsing moments, her body relaxed, accommodating his girth.

It was what he'd needed.

Fingers digging into the soft flesh of her ass hard enough to bruise, he drew back to the tip and surged forward again, and again, and again with deep, devastating thrusts.

Agonizing pleasure threatened to sweep him immediately away, but he held it at bay, needing to indulge in this insatiable perversion he'd developed for his wife. He held her hair in an unyielding grip as he surged forward, feeling every feminine muscle clenching around his shaft.

"Eli," she gasped.

He barely heard her over the sounds of his hips slapping against her ass. Of hard, wet flesh pistoning against tight, wet flesh.

He bent over her, curling his wide shoulders against her slim ones, stinging into her with swift curls of his spine. "Don't ask me to stop," he growled, though it escaped closer to a plea than he'd intended.

"No," she said around a tight whimper. "No. I'm going to… It's coming. I'm afraid I'll…I'll scream."

Fuck if that wasn't the hottest thing she'd ever said.

Eli covered her open mouth just in time. She buried a strangled cry against the rough skin, then another as she bucked back against him. Twisting and writhing, pulling and arching as her intimate muscles clenched and pulsed.

He fought his own release valiantly, and won, too, until her sharp little teeth bit into the fleshy pad of his palm.

The pain seared him so sweetly, he barely had the time to clamp down on his own thunderous cry, nearly biting off his tongue in order to do so.

Never had he felt a climax so completely. So intricately. From his own seed leaving his body, jettisoning her womb before he sank so deep, he touched the edge. It pulled from him in confounding surges, like waves breaching the shore and crawling higher than they dared before.

Finally, his pleasure ebbed, and he dropped his forehead between her shoulder blades.

She pressed a soft kiss against the indents her teeth

had left in his palm, and the tenderness in the gesture threatened to unstitch him.

A tremor undulated down her spine, passing between their joined flesh and licking his own back with electric pleasure.

It was like being released from chains he'd worn for damn near four days. Andromeda had nothing on him, as he'd have preferred literal chains to the ones she held over his soul. "I'd better make peace with this now," he lamented breathlessly. "Doesn't matter how hard I try to be free of this, I will never be able to give you up."

It was Rosaline who disengaged from him, moving as far as she could in the confined space to straighten and smooth her skirts back down her legs. As he tucked himself back in his trousers, she bent at the knees to retrieve her ripped undergarments before facing him.

"How hard did you try to be free of me?" she asked, her voice dull between her own beleaguered breaths.

Smoothing down his hair, Eli castigated himself for making it sound worse than he'd meant it, but he answered her honestly. "That morning I left, I'd almost convinced myself I wouldn't return..."

"Because of our predicament." Her shadow shifted, and he wished like hell he could see her face. "The predicament *I* put us in."

"Because you stole the chalice and lied to me about it for weeks. *Weeks.* While I tore this world apart looking for it." He turned from her, his hand landing on the latch of the closet. Why the fuck were they hiding in here, anyhow? They'd done nothing wrong.

"No one would blame you, if you went back home to America," she said tersely. "It's very probable you will feel less trapped there in all that wide open space. Don't they call it the land of the free?"

And just like that, his warm afterglow flared into a temper. "Don't act like your life wouldn't be easier without me to keep an eye on your sticky fingers. I'm not the thief here. *I'm* not the liar, or have you forgotten? I've done *nothing* to break faith."

She was silent for so long, their breaths became cannon blasts over a dark battlefield. He could sense her behind him. Close but not touching. Her heavy exhalations breaking against his spine.

They'd been as connected as two bodies could be only seconds ago. Hell, his orgasm still shimmered along his spine.

But there was a chasm growing between them he couldn't see his way across.

"You abandoned me for *days*," she accused in a voice so low he had to strain to hear it. "Left me with no word, no goodbye. You did that to be cruel. To hurt me, because I hurt you. But there's a difference between what we've done to each other, Eli. I *never* intended you any pain. Had I known how my actions affected you, I would have cut off my own hands to keep from offending you like I did. But you…you deserted our marriage without ever allowing me a voice. And now you've decided to return to our bed, because your lust will not allow you to leave your thief of a wife?"

"That isn't what I said."

"It's what you meant," she insisted.

"And what if it is? This thing you do, it isn't right. Why can't you just stop?"

"Don't you think I've *tried?*" she railed, her voice raising in both pitch and volume. "I don't want this. I would give anything not to be this way!"

At that, Eli paused, utterly confounded. "Then…why?"

"I wish I knew." She was back to barely above a whisper now, a bleak thread reaching through the dark to lance him with her pain. "It started when I was nine. This…this overwhelming need. I would have such fits, such bouts of pure physical suffering. My chest would feel like it might explode, my skin would be raw, my lungs refusing to work. The doctor said it was nerves. Tried to dose me with all sorts of tonics, but nothing worked... At least not well. The first time I took something, it was after my mother had berated me for an eternity. The relief I felt was indescribable, and so then next time I was in trouble, I did it again. And again. And each time I did...I'd gain control over the sensations threatening to rip my heart from my chest."

Eli swallowed around a lump of sympathy. Caleb had suffered something like she described. Conniptions of heart palpitations and uncontrollable shaking. Especially in times of stress. He'd become convinced that he couldn't breathe. That his throat was closing over. They went to the doctor several times, only to be told he was fine.

But he wasn't fine...

"Does your family know? Does Morley?"

She shook her head. "Don't blame Morley, he has no idea."

"I was asking if anyone ever offered to find you help... Did no one else realize? Your mother, or father?"

"Only my Uncle Reginald, but..." She shifted again, her shadow becoming smaller. "He...he made it worse."

"The fuck did he do?" Eli demanded, his entire being screaming at the stars to not let his dark suspicion be true.

"I'd stopped for a while, after finishing school," she remembered aloud. "Emmaline and I realized that I seemed to get worse during times of stress, and if I cultivated other behaviors, I could keep the need at bay...but then Father stopped coming to visit often, and Uncle Reginald moved in with us at Fairhaven."

"Did he touch you...where he shouldn't?" Eli asked from between clenched teeth.

She exhaled slowly, and his heart shriveled at the

stress he heard in the sound. "Not in the way you mean. Not really. He'd a cane we all detested by the time he was killed, and he used it on me the most. As a rapping reminder against my shoulder blades to remind me to keep my posture. As a painful snap against the hand if Emmaline or I were to eat more than he'd portioned for us. Sometimes, he'd lift my skirts with it, claiming to examine whether or not I'd properly situated my underthings."

Eli didn't allow his teeth to unclench, so he couldn't threaten to kill the perverted fuck. Again.

"He made it clear every single day that he was crafting me into his idea of the perfect woman," she continued. "Assiduously clean. Endlessly elegant. Words never above a whisper. Footsteps never heavier than an autumn leaf's fall. He spoke to me of things he ought not to. Happened upon me while bathing or dressing, and then punished me for impropriety. He never touched me. Not with his hands. He treated other people as if they were filthy, and shrank from physical contact. I suppose I should be grateful… But there *was* a malevolent light in his eyes when he punished me. And it was not unlike the sexual interest of other men.

"He enjoyed it, my pain. My humiliation. *That* was what he craved. What he lusted for. He watched me so very closely in order to catch me in any crime against the family's extraordinary strictures, so that he could be the one to mete out my consequence."

Eli realized now why she'd such an intense reaction to his threat to do the self-same thing.

"Living under such intense regard seems to exacerbate my proclivity. Indeed, often the anticipation of punishment would drive me to steal. Little things. His shaving brush. A favorite Bible. A pair of spectacles. The black bishop off the chess set in his study. He'd caught me once, at seventeen, swiping a brass button from a shop in town.

Rather than have me return the pilfered item, he gave me five sharp swats with the ruler on the open palm of my hand. When my skin broke and bled upon the final blow, I noticed how…" Her breath hitched and she swallowed convulsively. "I noticed how aroused he'd become, and I fled the house.

"I was caught, of course, and became little better than a prisoner in my own home. I'd taken to stealing things from my siblings, from the staff, and from Uncle Reginald when I had no alternative and could no longer stand it. I hardly ate. I never slept. I was a ghost waiting for this… this monster inside me to finally do me in for good. My mother died, and then my father and his counterfeit Baroness, leaving everything to Felicity. Uncle Reginald was so livid, he enacted a plan to murder Felicity, and was subsequently thwarted and…killed by her husband, thank God."

"Jesus…"

"After all of that, I'll admit I was perilously close to… to giving up. I'd a plan to climb to the top of Fairhaven and pitch myself off the roof. But then, the Goodes gave Emmett his title, and invited us into their house. Into their family. And for a while, I was happy. I was *better*. I was better, until Emmett's fiancée and her mother stayed at our home. She is so hateful to poor Emmett. So critical of everything and…that night when I crept into the observatory, I really did only mean to use the telescope. But my demon scratched and scratched at me, and as I looked over your treasure, I took the thing that seemed the least valuable. And then I lied about it so no one would find out. So that Emmett wouldn't lose everything. And that…that is how we came to be in this predicament."

By the time she finished, Eli felt as if he'd swallowed an entire sack of nails, so cutting was his guilt. So sharp was his rage.

"Perhaps I should have pitched myself off the roof of Fairhaven, after all," she whispered.

Reaching for her, he opened his mouth to protest at the exact time someone opened the door to the closet, startling them both.

"I thought I heard voices in here."

Whirling, Eli found himself eye to eye-patch with the one and only Dorian Blackwell. Sleek as a witch's black cat, and every bit as sinister, the so-called King of the London Underworld sized up the tableau before him immediately.

Likely aided by the undergarments clutched in his wife's hands.

"Mr. Wolfe," Blackwell said with a mischievous half-grin. "And Mrs. Wolfe, I presume?"

Eli glanced over his shoulder in time to see his wife whisk her torn underthings behind her back. "Oh," she gasped breathlessly. "Pardon the intrusion, my lord, we'd heard something was missing and—erm—thought to help search for it."

"Indeed?" Blackwell lifted the dark brow over his one good eye. "Well, that's terribly kind of you, Mrs. Wolfe. My wife also has a penchant for pulling me into a hidden corner for a *thorough* searching."

Eli coughed, his cheeks heating even through the shared look of approving masculine commiseration.

"Speaking of searching," Blackwell continued. "There has been a theft...though the owner of the item has decided not to divulge what exactly was taken. The story is it was pilfered by a woman, and so the ladies are gathering in the great hall to be searched before they are allowed to leave. In case the story is false, the men will be searched in the kitchens and expelled through the servant's entrance. We've decided to call off the auction for now."

Dark suspicion threaded through Eli's guts, and he

turned slowly, afraid to find guilt splashed all over his wife's face.

What he found, was something so brilliant and terrible, he couldn't decide if it was pain, fear, or anger.

"I'll, erm, leave you two to compose yourselves," Blackwell said as the light disappeared behind the closed door.

Eli waited for the footsteps to recede before asking, "Rosaline, was it you?" He needed to know in order to protect her from the consequences and get her away from here as quickly as possible.

"Yes," she hissed in the voice women sometimes used that made it impossible to tell between truth and sarcasm. "Yes, Eli. I *am* an insatiable thief, after all. But out of everything I've taken, I regret this most of all."

With that, she dashed around him and burst through the door, but not before shoving her undergarments into his hands.

Stunned, Eli watched her march down the hall with her head held high, even as so many of her tresses had been loosened by his rough grip and cascaded down her back.

Still half-drained of sense after such an ecstatic interlude, followed by the intensity of her recollection, he gaped down at the garments in his hands, blinking with bewilderment. He went into that closet a martyr, and emerged the villain... What now? How did he fix this?

As if by magic, Blackwell appeared with something that looked like a doctor's satchel. He opened it, offering the empty space to him. "It appears that in your hasty—were we calling it a search?—you've relieved your poor wife of her entire...rigging."

Eli glanced between it and the lethal blackguard next to him. He'd stripped her of garters, clasps, ribbons, and everything, tore them right off her tender flesh. No wonder the wad of delicate clothing was heavier than expected.

"If you place them in here, you may retrieve the satchel from the butler's office after you've been cleared to leave," Dorian offered, shaking the satchel as if to prompt him to hurry.

"Thank you, kindly." Eli gracelessly stuffed it all inside the bag and snapped it closed, not liking his wife's under-things exposed to another man's eyes.

Er...eye, on account of him only having the one.

"Think nothing of it, Mr. Wolfe. Now this way, if you please."

Eli spent the wait milling over the words his wife had hurled at him. Grinding them down to examine their contents, to examine it for a vein of truth in the grit of the emotion. He barely felt the search, spreading his arms and legs in a Vitruvian stance while a stoic man patted him in places no other man had dared venture.

"Easy there, bucko," he warned. "None of your counterparts better dare to touch my wife like that, or you'll be sucking on the barrel of my pistol."

"Not to worry," drawled the older Scottish gentleman with kind blue eyes. "The lasses will be searched by a woman."

"All right, then," Eli nodded, wishing he felt better. That he didn't fear what they might find.

By the time he was cleared, it was all Eli could do not to sprint from Northwalk Hall in search of Rosaline.

"Mr. Wolfe!" the butler called, puffing after him. "Mr. Wolfe! You've forgotten your satchel."

Whirling, Eli took the bag and thanked the butler. "Do you know if the ladies are finished?"

"The ones who are should be waiting in the drive." The butler pointed around to the front where a mess of carriages awaited the mass exodus. "I've been told to inform you that Mrs. Wolfe was among the first searched, and was seen hiring a hansom to conduct her away."

Cursing, he sprinted for his carriage.

Her eyes had been so raw, her expression so wounded and bleak. A part of him worried she might do herself a mischief.

A picture of her standing on the ledge of Hespera House caused him to push his driver aside and snatch the reins from him.

Whipping the coach into a bracing run over the cobbles, he chanted her name much in the same way he'd done on the night he'd pulled Caleb's dead body from the rubble.

He wasn't a praying man, but this time he sent a plea to every deity he'd ever heard of, even the devil himself, promising his very soul if only he could make it to her in time.

CHAPTER 14

Rosaline stared up at the stars, her arms flung wide on the damp grass, her legs numb, and her feet fallen open.

In all her time here, she'd never much noticed the gardens at Hespera House. Now that she was unable to move, she wondered if she'd ever leave them.

Bury me here, she thought, *beneath the rare winter stars.*

It felt as though the dreary winter sky had cleared suddenly...as if the heavens heard her soul's weary sob and sparkled for her benefit.

How many nights had she stared up at the stars, lonely tears leaking from her eyes, speaking to the constellations as if they were familiar friends?

Even when she'd known better.

Tonight was her last night with this particular sky... She'd never see it again. Some people believed their fates were already written in the stars.

She fervently hoped that was not true. Because she was a blight to all who crossed her path, and her own fate was both confusing and callous.

Though her body was deliciously bruised and her heart bleeding, she also swam in this strange, euphoric sense of relief. She'd told the truth. All of it. And the unburdening of it had made her feel as though she might survive this.

She'd handed Eli his sapphire to do with as he pleased, and now there was nothing between them but the truth of who she was and what she'd done.

The stars would decide what happened next.

A commotion filtered through the silence of the evening, doors slamming and her husband's voice carrying through the halls with all of his unfettered American ruckus.

Smiling fondly to herself, she closed her eyes, listening to the tempestuous resonance of the man she wanted to have, but who would never be able to trust her.

Cruel, cruel stars.

The garden door slammed open, and Rosaline forgot to breathe.

Not an hour ago, he'd been inside her. And the desperate passion of that act had given her hope. A hope he'd crushed with the first words out of his mouth.

She didn't want to face his wrath again. Not tonight. She simply couldn't bear—

"Rosaline." He choked out her name as running footfalls skidded to a halt beside her. She lifted an eyelid in time to see him hit his knees and scoop her up against his chest. "Rosaline. Honey. Breathe, damn you. No. No. No."

Squirming in his tight hold, she pressed against the steely muscle beneath his jacket. "I can't very well breathe if you're smothering me with your chest."

His arms went slack, and she fell back to the ground in a heap.

"Ow."

"Shit, shit, sorry!" He reached for her, then paused, as if he couldn't decide where his hands should go. "What have you done?" he asked, his eyes so wild she could see the whites. "Did you drink something? Did you jump?"

"What are you talking about?" She sat up, wriggling toes gone numb from the cold.

"You said you should have jumped from the roof at Fairhaven." He looked up toward the ledge upon which their entire fate had been set in motion.

"And you thought I'd return home and hurl myself from *our* roof?" She scowled at him. "What sort of fool do you take me for?"

He sat back on his haunches, pale as a ghost, staring at her as if she'd sprouted horns. "You were lying here still as a corpse, not breathing, on an icy December night, what the hell was I supposed to think?"

"That I was stargazing." She pointed up to the astonishingly clear sky, cleansed by a week's worth of freezing rain.

"Stargazing." He closed his eyes as if he needed not to look at her for a moment. "Of fucking course, you were. Jesus Josephat Christ, woman, you can't just—"

"What is this?" she interrupted as her foot caught on an upended leather satchel.

"Blackwell thought it best I didn't parade through his guests waving the underkit you shoved at me, so he lent me this to hide them in."

Rosaline gasped. Released a broken laugh. Then another as she grappled with the satchel's buckles. "Did you find it?" she asked. "Have you opened it?"

"No, I didn't have time to sniff your drawers between being searched for a thief and racing home to make sure I didn't find you in a sprawled heap on the ground," he groused.

"Eli," she said with an excited breath as she rose to her knees and grappled with the lace and cotton drawers until she found the seam in which she'd tucked the treasure.

His treasure.

Extracting the sapphire, she offered it to him with

both hands, transfixed by the deep blue beauty of the rough-cut stone.

He stared at it. Not blinking. No muscle twitching. No expression at all.

"I overheard you telling the Duchesse it'd been taken from you," she said, encouraging him to take it by sliding it closer. "I thought... I don't know what I thought. I just wanted you to have the treasure that meant so much to you. The one you and your brother spent a lifetime searching for."

Eli rose to his own knees, snatching the gem from her outstretched hand.

To her everlasting astonishment, he tossed it on the ground without giving it a second glance.

"I came to this country searching for one fortune." He lifted his hands to her face, cupping it as if it were the most fragile, precious thing in the world. "But I realize what I found was something more valuable than I could ever imagine."

She swallowed as her heart leapt into her chest, not trusting the brilliant shine chasing the shadows away from his dark eyes. Could he truly mean...?

"Rosaline. My little wife. My greatest treasure." He pulled her close, burying his face in her hair, cupping her head gently as she rested her cheek on his shoulder and finally allowed her tears to flow.

"Forgive me, honey, for being like them. Like every person who was supposed to love you, and instead made you feel small and afraid. It was their job to protect you, not turn your sanctuary into a place where you had no safe space to be yourself. No control over who you were or what happened to you. Nothing but censure and perverse expectations." He pulled back enough to gaze down at her, and what she read in his eyes made the tears fall even harder.

He thumbed away her tears, only to have the river overflow his efforts. "Don't cry, honey. I've got you."

"That's why I'm weeping," she explained through hiccupping sobs. "I want this so much, but how can you ever trust me? I am still so…broken."

"We're all broken, Rosaline," he said, his rough features softened with compassion. "I've always been a harsh bastard who tends to come out swinging rather than talking. And that kind of thing is sometimes necessary with bullheaded miners." He lifted her chin as was his habit and kissed away the salt of her tears. "But you're my wife. I took a vow to honor and protect you. To cherish you… and that means I got to try to listen. To understand you. And if I don't understand, to do my best to help you in any way I can."

She sniffed, as some of her despair was washed away by his words. Her fingers lifted to his dear face, tracing the brackets next to his hard mouth, scraping on his beloved shadow beard.

"I'm sorry for running off like I did," he said, turning his cheek to nuzzle into her palm. "I think I knew deep down somewhere that if I stayed, I'd forgive you. That I'd hand you this hard heart and let you crush it if you wanted to. And, like a coward, I fled. From the fact that not only could you betray me like Beau had done, but I was becoming such a fool for you, I'd lie down and let you stomp all over my pride, my honor, my fucking dignity, such as it is in this country." The crooked grin he offered her melted away the last of her tears, and she flung her arms around him, driving him to the ground.

"Easy there, honey, I'm an old man. I don't know if I'm ready for another round just yet."

She kissed him with all the love she could hold, which was more than most people twice her size. "I promise to be better," she whispered against his mouth. "I will always be honest with you, Eli. Starting with this first confession."

He tensed a bit beneath her, but his gaze was steady as he looked up at her.

"I love you, Elijah Wolfe."

"Oh, honey." He lifted his hand to extract the last of the pins from her ruined hair, so it could cascade over them both in cool waves of silk. "You took the words right out of my mouth."

"Then here," she whispered. "Have them back again." Her lips sealed over his, and that seal didn't break even when he sat up, lifted her against him, and stood.

"Come to bed, little wife," he ordered with a smile, nuzzling her nose with his own. "It's your job to keep my toes warm in this ridiculous, eternally chilly country."

"It's a wifely duty I take very seriously," she whispered against his neck.

He almost dropped her a second time when she nibbled the tip of his ear.

"Dammit, woman, you'll be the death of me," he muttered.

"I hope not," she murmured against his warm, fragrant skin. "I intend to be married to you for a *very* long time."

EPILOGUE

A YEAR LATER

Rosaline knew she needed to give up the precious sleeping child in her arms. After fourteen hours of labor, she felt exhaustion's pull threatening her consciousness.

But how could she miss a single moment, when they were so perfect?

All her fingers. All her toes. The wealth of hair as dark as the man who'd gathered them both in his arms, upsetting the very British midwife, who wanted fathers to have exactly nothing to do with the birth.

"What should we name her?" she queried around a yawn.

"Honeysuckle?" he offered.

"Be serious."

"I was being serious," he muttered, portending effrontery.

"What about Charity?" she offered. "It would fit in with so many of the Goode names."

"Nu-uh," he declined vehemently. "No virtues, and no names ending in 'line' or starting with 'Emm.' I already have a hell of a time with Caroline, Rosaline, Emmaline, Emmett. No. Just no."

"And why not a virtue?" she asked.

"Have you met your sisters?" He counted them off on his fingers. "Prudence is impetuous. Mercy is ruthless. Felicity is serious. And Honoria well...she's all right, I guess."

Rosaline couldn't help but let laughter shake the child, and was so grateful when she didn't wake.

"Name our kid Charity and she'll be a miser and a cheat," he continued. "Name her Chastity, and...well, I don't have to spell that one out for you."

Rosaline let her giggles die with a contented sigh, her head lolling against his chest. "This is more difficult than I thought."

"What about Courtney?" he offered.

She wrinkled her nose. "I dislike it immediately."

"It's my middle name."

"Oh, well...I suppose we could consider—"

This time, it was his chest that shook with laughter. "I love you, woman."

"What if we name her for one of our favorite places from our honeymoon? Maybe Florence or Vienna?"

"I dislike that immediately." He threw her words back at her.

"Are we about to have our first row?"

"She's just so perfect. She's the most perfect child to have ever been born, don't you think?"

"I know exactly what to call her."

"What's that?"

"Andromeda."

"You two are everything in my sky."

Though she still loved to map the stars, her eyes did not search them as often as they used to. And when her fingers itched to take, which was less and less these days, he was there to hold her hand. To quiet the vibrations. And, sometimes, to find a solution that could ease both her suffering, and still keep her from being a thief. Yes, she looked at the stars less, because what mattered was right here. Whatever strange substance had crafted the universe and all its mysteries, her husband held it in his eyes as he looked at her.

"Andromeda," she murmured. "Our little constellation of joy. She's going to slay her own demons, I think."

He passed his hand over the downy head. "If so, she'll have learned it from her mama."

They pressed their foreheads together for a precious moment, and as Rosaline began to give over to sleep, she felt the tiny weight of their child lifted from her chest.

"Come here, little mite," he crooned. "Let's let Mama sleep. You've both had a rough couple of hours, huh? Why don't you sit here and tell me all about it?"

Rosaline didn't want to miss this precious moment, but she released her grip on consciousness, knowing that life would be here when she awoke, and so would the family she loved.

ALSO BY KERRIGAN BYRNE

A Goode Girls Romance

Seducing a Stranger

Courting Trouble

Dancing With Danger

Tempting Fate

Crying Wolfe

Making Merry

The Business of Blood Series

The Business of Blood

A Treacherous Trade

A Vocation of Violence

Victorian Rebels

The Highwayman

The Hunter

The Highlander

The Duke

The Scot Beds His Wife

The Duke With the Dragon Tattoo

The Earl on the Train

The MacLauchlan Berserkers

Highland Secret

Highland Shadow

Highland Stranger

To Seduce a Highlander

The MacKay Banshees

Highland Darkness

Highland Devil

Highland Destiny

To Desire a Highlander

The de Moray Druids

Highland Warlord

Highland Witch

Highland Warrior

To Wed a Highlander

Contemporary Suspense

A Righteous Kill

Also by Kerrigan

How to Love a Duke in Ten Days

All Scot And Bothered

ABOUT THE AUTHOR

Kerrigan Byrne is the USA Today Bestselling and award winning author of several novels in both the romance and mystery genre.

She lives on the Olympic Peninsula in Washington with her two Rottweiler mix rescues and one very clingy cat. When she's not writing and researching, you'll find her on the beach, kayaking, or on land eating, drinking, shopping, and attending live comedy, ballet, or too many movies.

Kerrigan loves to hear from her readers! To contact her or learn more about her books, please visit her site or find her on most social media platforms: www.kerriganbyrne.com